"Are you all right?"

Casey called to Finnick as he stumbled from the smashed-up truck.

But suddenly the barn lights switched off, plunging everything into darkness.

A figure slammed into her, sending her crashing onto the wooden floor. Strong hands clamped around her throat and squeezed. She grabbed at them, trying desperately to ease the grip on her neck. Her body thrashed as she tried to throw the attacker off her. A scream for help ripped through her lungs.

"Finnick!" she shouted, throwing every bit of fear, strength and hope she had into the word. "Help!"

Help me, Lord! Save my life!

Her attacker's grip heightened until it hurt to breathe. Darkness swam before her eyes.

"Shut up or I'll kill you!" The man leaned toward her. His voice was harsh and artificially deep, like he was afraid she'd recognize it. "Where is he? Is he here?"

Was he looking for her late husband, Tim?

"No..." She tried to shout the word, but all she could manage was to whisper. "He's...dead..."

"If you're hiding him, Casey," the man hissed, "I will find him...and then kill you both."

Maggie K. Black is an award-winning journalist and romantic suspense author with an insatiable love of traveling the world. She has lived in the American South, Europe and the Middle East. She now makes her home in Canada with her history-teacher husband, their two beautiful girls and a small but mighty dog. Maggie enjoys connecting with her readers at maggiekblack.com.

Books by Maggie K. Black

Love Inspired Suspense

Undercover Protection
Surviving the Wilderness
Her Forgotten Life
Cold Case Chase
Undercover Baby Rescue

Mountain Country K-9 Unit

Crime Scene Secrets

Unsolved Case Files

Cold Case Tracker
Christmas Cold Case

Visit the Author Profile page
at LoveInspired.com for more titles.

Christmas Cold Case

MAGGIE K. BLACK

Love Inspired SUSPENSE

INSPIRATIONAL ROMANCE

LOVE INSPIRED® SUSPENSE
INSPIRATIONAL ROMANCE

ISBN-13: 978-1-335-48393-5

Christmas Cold Case

Love Inspired
22 Adelaide St. West, 41st Floor
Toronto, Ontario M5H 4E3, Canada
www.LoveInspired.com

Printed in U.S.A.

Recycling programs for this product may not exist in your area.

And thou shalt have joy and gladness;
and many shall rejoice at his birth.
—*Luke* 1:14

To Kripke and Bernadette
of Sonora

and their photographer
Teresa Anne Murphy

For all the joy your pictures have brought to my life

ONE

It was like driving through a thick, vanilla milkshake that was somehow still in the blender. Inspector Ethan Finnick navigated his pickup van through the storm, as thick globs of snow pelted from the darkness and splattered his windshield. He drove slowly across the narrow, one-lane swing bridge that connected Manitoulin Island to the mainland. Narrow iron bars rose on either side.

"Doesn't exactly feel safe, does it?" Finnick asked, glancing in the rearview mirror at his constant back seat companion, an elderly black Labrador retriever named Nippy.

Nippy—short for Nipissing—had technically retired from his job as a K-9 cadaver dog six weeks ago when Finnick had stepped down as head of the RCMP's Ontario K-9 Unit to head up the country's first Cold Case Task Force. But as far as Finnick was concerned, the two of them were partners for life. The vehicle shuddered over a bump and Nippy woofed in complaint before lying his grizzled snout back down on his paws.

Finnick snorted. Then he prayed for strength and wisdom to face what awaited him on the other side of the bridge.

Casey Thompson.

Unbidden, the beautiful heart-shaped face and fierce hazel eyes he'd last seen some ten years ago filled his mind. Instinctively, he pushed the memory away as quickly and ineffectually as the wipers currently trying to keep the snow off his windshield. Casey's former husband, Tim, was suspected of murdering a college student named Stella Neilson a decade ago, and Casey was the potential key to solving the cold case now. The Ontario police commissioner himself had asked that Finnick's new team make this case a top priority due to how police had bungled the original investigation.

Finnick eased the van off the single-lane swing bridge and drove past a long line of other drivers waiting to cross in the other direction and get off the island once the light changed. Hopefully, he'd be headed that way too before long. He turned south toward the small town of Juniper Cove.

Finnick had been in his late thirties when he'd first met Casey. His hair had already been going gray back then, and he'd gone by *Finnick* for so long, he'd almost forgotten that technically his first name was Ethan. Casey had been in her late twenties, with somehow both the idealism of a person half her age and the wisdom of someone twice it. Needless to say, he'd liked being around her. Nippy had just been a pup fresh out of K-9 training when they'd been sent up from Toronto for a few days. They'd been tasked with searching Casey's sprawling Manitoulin property for any trace of her missing husband and nineteen-year-old Stella, who'd last been seen leaving the island together. They'd found nothing.

When, seven years after Tim and Stella's disappearance, Casey had successfully petitioned the court to declare Tim dead so that she could collect his life insurance, a lot of people in law enforcement cried foul.

But, so help me, Lord, there's something about this case that's stuck under my skin like a splinter I can't reach. When we met ten years ago, she'd seemed so strong in her conviction that Tim couldn't be a killer. Not to mention her faith that You'd see justice done, despite the chaos battering her life. Show me the truth beneath the lies. Help me convince Casey to assist us in finally solving what happened to Tim and Stella.

It had hardly been Finnick and Nippy's

first case and they'd worked countless ones since.

Yet when he'd learned the case was being reopened and that Casey was reluctant to talk, he'd felt the urge to jump into his van and drive the six-hour trek from Toronto to try for himself.

"So now I'm going to drop by and talk to her in person," Finnick told the dog in the back seat, as if Nippy had been listening in on his conflicted thoughts. "Worse she can do is slam the door in my face, right?"

He was less than twenty minutes away, and maybe he should give her an opportunity to slam the phone down before he showed up at her house unannounced. He was about to instruct his hand's-free feature to call Casey's number when his phone rang, shattering the silence.

He punched the accept button. "Hello?"

"It's Jackson," came a deep male voice. "Hudson and I are calling you to give you some really good news. We've decided to take up your offer to join the team."

K-9 Officer Jackson Locke and his German shepherd partner, Hudson, had served with Finnick for years and had been among the first job offers he'd made for the new Cold Case Task Force. Formerly of the RCMP, Jackson made five, joining his sister, private eye Gemma Locke, Constable Caleb Perry and K-9 Officer Lucas Harper of the special investigations unit along with his arson-detecting yellow Lab, Michigan.

Thank You, Lord. My team is coming together.

Finnick had always taken an interest in cold cases, wanting justice for victims and families who were still waiting for it. It had been a long-held dream of his to form this unit, and now that dream was becoming a reality.

"So, brief me," Jackson said. "Gemma said you've already started on our first case?"

Finnick replied, "Nippy and I just arrived on Manitoulin Island and I'm on my way to talk to Casey Thompson since the cold case involves her late husband… She may be reluctant to help though."

"Can't really blame her," Gemma's voice echoed down the line, and Finnick realized he was on speaker. "We're basically asking her to go before the courts and announce she just might be wrong about whether or not her late husband is dead. The past ten and a half years can't have been easy for her. A lot of amateur online sleuths think Casey helped Tim kill a woman and cover up the crime, and then killed him too."

"And the internet is never wrong about anything," Jackson said, dryly.

Gemma snorted. While Jackson was a cop through and through, Gemma was the team's lone civilian, a PI and a meticulously focused researcher who matched her brother's talent beat for beat. She was Finnick's first hire for the new task force.

"Long story short," Gemma said, "eleven years ago, Stella Neilson was living on Manitoulin Island and engaged to marry the island's golden boy, Drew Thatcher. He now runs a real estate business."

Finnick slowed the van to a crawl and rounded a curve. He was less than fifteen minutes away from Casey's home now. In between the sheets of blowing snow, he could now see Juniper Cove spread out below him in a blurry tapestry of Christmas lights. He blinked and still saw colored dots dancing before his eyes. A brightly decorated sign loomed above him. "Welcome to Juniper Cove, Finalist for Canada's Most Whimsical Christmas Village. Sponsored by Thatcher Family Real Estate, the Perfect Home for the Perfect Family."

Speaking of Drew Thatcher... Despite that Stella's fiancé might normally be a person of interest in a case like this, Drew's supervisor at work had provided him with an ironclad alibi back then and he'd been cleared of any wrongdoing.

"Stella and Tim worked together at the local hardware store," Gemma went on, filling her brother in. "He was her supervisor. Stella disappeared a few months before the wedding, and the last time she was seen alive was leaving the island in the front seat of Tim's car. Apparently, it was bright red and hard to miss."

The snow was growing even thicker in front of his eyes now. He slowed further, not wanting to miss his next turn.

"They both vanished," Gemma said. "There was a rumored sighting of the pair in Sudbury a few weeks later, but it was never proved to be them."

"And what about the original detective assigned to the case?" Jackson asked.

"He died a few years ago and the case was just left to gather dust," Finnick said. "We've got his files and they're really weak. He was convinced Stella ran away with Tim. I barely met the man. My only involvement in the case was a search of Casey's property with Nippy. And that was a full year after Tim and Stella had gone missing."

Which was how he'd ended up sitting across from Casey in her farmhouse kitchen, touching her hand and feeling like he'd just somehow found something special buried deep in her eyes that he'd never even known that he'd wanted to find.

And that he wasn't about to let himself act on.

"Now, you are coming for Christmas Eve dinner, right, Finnick?" Gemma asked, breaking into his thoughts. "Because both Caleb and Lucas have confirmed, and with Jackson here, we'll have the full team."

"Sure," Finnick said, making a right onto Casey's street. He wasn't really in the habit of celebrating Christmas, but it would be good to get the team together before the task force launched in January.

"The storm's getting worse by the second and I'm nearly there. I'll call you back." They said their goodbyes and he disconnected.

Finnick still wanted to give Casey the heads-up he was coming. He commanded his hand's-free app to select her number.

"Finnick," Casey said. She'd answered before it even finished ringing once. "I'm on the roof of my barn, trying to fix a twisted string of Christmas lights. Can I call you back?"

She's on the roof fixing Christmas lights in this weather?

"What?" The word exploded from his lungs more as an exclamation than a question.

He could hear the wind rushing down the phone line, echoing the wail of it outside his van, along with some kind of rattling sound. He had no doubt she was telling the truth.

"I'm on the roof—"

"—of your barn, I heard!" he said and

remembered that Casey ran an online business making handmade soaps and candles out of her converted barn-slash-garage. "Climb down and I'll talk to you on the ground."

For a moment, there was no answer but the whistling wind and a clattering sound he guessed was the twisted string of lights. In all the time he'd thought about one day talking to Casey again, this had never once been how he'd imagined it.

"Hang on," she said. "I'm just making my way to the trap door. Don't worry, I made sure I was tethered to the drop ladder before I came out."

Well, at least she hadn't climbed a ladder up the side of the building.

"Why did you even answer the phone if you're on the roof?" he asked.

"Because I saw your name on the screen," she said, "I was afraid the call would drop, and I don't know how long it's going to be before we lose cell service in this storm. Phone service isn't exactly reliable here and it's actually best at the top of the barn."

But his personal number was unlisted and so it shouldn't have shown up on call display. Then it hit him. She must've kept it saved in her phone all these years.

His heart skipped an unfamiliar beat. She'd answered *because* it was him.

"Nippy and I are on our way to see you," he started.

"If this is about this new Cold Case Task Force thing, I need more time to think about it. It's a really big decision."

"I'm the head of the task force thing," he said. "I'm looking into Tim and Stella's disappearance, and the Ontario police commissioner has personally asked me to see if we can overturn Tim's death."

"Tim's dead!" Her voice rose above the wind. "He didn't hurt Stella and I'm not going to help you prove otherwise. Besides, I used the insurance money to pay off his family's debts. This farm has been in his family for four generations.

If I declare him alive now, the insurance company will sue me and I'll lose Tim's family's farm."

Well, regrettably, it wasn't up to her.

"Hey! Hey! Get away from there!" she shouted suddenly, her voice aimed away from the phone now, and it took him a moment to register that he wasn't the one she was shouting at. "Finnick, I've got to go, I think there's a trespasser on my property trying to break into my shed—"

A loud banging noise cut off the final word from her lips.

"Casey!" he shouted, feeling something lurch in his chest as her name exploded from his lips. "Are you okay?"

But the phone had gone dead, and when he tried back over and over again, all he got was the incessant beeping sound of an incomplete call. His heart seemed to thud along with the sound.

Lord, please help Casey! Take care and keep her safe until I can get there.

Wind beat harder against the side of the

van, colluding with the ice beneath his tires to try to send him flying into a ditch. Everything inside him wanted to speed to Casey's farm to find out why the call had dropped and make sure she was okay. Instead, he gritted his teeth and focused on keeping his vehicle on the road. He must be close now.

The snow fell harder, but finally, he glimpsed Casey's farm. Her house and barn were wrapped in lights. What appeared to be a life-size nativity scene stretched across the entire front of her property.

All of a sudden, a young woman who he'd never seen before dashed out in front of his van so abruptly that Finnick cried out to God for help and smashed his foot on the brake. The van slid, trying to gain traction as the woman stood in shock, like a rabbit caught in headlights.

Fragile—with long pale hair tossed by the wind and eyes huge with fear. His eyes darted to the small bundle she was clutching to her chest.

Hang on, is she holding a baby?

His brakes locked. His van spun wildly.

He was careening toward her with no way to stop.

His phone flew free from its dashboard mount and clattered somewhere behind him.

"Get down, Nippy!" he shouted to his K-9 partner. "Brace for impact!"

Finnick gripped the steering wheel so hard his knuckles ached.

Save us, Lord! Please don't let me hit her!

Then he was flying off the road through a field and into the snow. He heard a thud and realized he'd hit something, just in time to catch a fleeting glimpse of a large, four-legged creature bouncing off his windshield. A wall of snow rushed up to meet him. Then came a bone-shattering crunch as the van smashed into something hard hidden under the snow. He was thrown against the seat belt. The airbags deployed. His windshield cracked and caved in.

And then it was over and silence fell. He couldn't hear the woman he'd nearly hit or the child she might've been holding.

"Nippy!" he called. "Are you okay?"

As for himself, he was sure to have aches and pains later, but nothing worth worrying about now. He wrestled with his seat belt, it fell free and then he twisted around to look into the back seat. Nippy scrambled up from the floor and licked his hand reassuringly. Finnick yanked his hood up, shoved the door open, then stepped out into the storm. He sunk into snow up to his knees. Nippy leaped into the front seat and climbed out, appearing unharmed. Sparkling Christmas lights that seemed to cover every inch of Casey's farmhouse and barn cast an odd ethereal glow over the snow. Thankfully, the object that had bounced off his van was some kind of camel that'd been part of a sprawling nativity scene. He didn't see the young woman with the baby anywhere.

"Hello?" he turned toward the road and shouted into the darkness. "Is anybody out there?"

The barn door flew open. There, in the golden light, stood the dark silhouette of Casey Thompson.

Tall and lithe, with her arms crossed and shoulder-length hair flying around her face.

"Finnick, is that you?" Casey's voice rang out through the darkness, brave and strong with only the tiniest hint of fear. "Are you all right?"

But as he opened his mouth to answer, a dark shadow moved behind her.

Then he heard Casey scream.

The figure had come out of nowhere, leaping from the shadows of the barn from somewhere behind her van, slamming into her body and throwing her back. Her feet slipped out from under her. Her body hit the floor. Then her attacker was on top of her. She couldn't make out his form, let alone his face. Strong hands clamped around her throat and squeezed. She grabbed at them, trying desperately to ease his grip on her neck as she thrashed about, struggling to throw him off her. A second scream for help ripped through her lungs, even as she felt her attacker squeezing her throat again.

"Finnick!" She shouted the name of the man she hoped had just crashed onto her property, throwing all the fear, strength and hope she had into the word. "Help!"

Help me, Lord! Save my life!

Her attacker's grip heightened until it hurt to breath. Darkness swam before her eyes. A second male voice shouted now, from somewhere on the edges of her consciousness. She couldn't make out his words. Then another sound reached her ears. A dog was barking, furiously.

"Shut up, sweet pea, or I'll kill you!" Her attacker leaned toward her. His voice was harsh and artificially deep, like he was afraid she'd recognize it. "Where is he? Is he here?"

He? He who?

Is he looking for Tim?

"No..." She tried to shout the word but all she could manage was to whisper, "He's...dead..."

The faint light of the Christmas bulbs outside the barn swam before her, and she finally saw the face of the man attacking her. It was a mask, rubbery and loose, of a shepherd with a supersized grin and yellow beard molded to his face. She blinked. He was wearing the very mask and robes she'd decked her scarecrow out in just a few days ago.

Her older sister had complained it was creepy.

Now, it was downright terrifying.

"If you're hiding him, Casey," the man hissed, "I will find him and kill you both."

The barking rose to a fever pitch.

"Get away from her!" Finnick's voice reached her ears.

The man in the creepy shepherd mask leaped off her. He ran into the dark recesses of her barn, no doubt to escape through the back door. She sat up and gasped quick and painful breaths, as her wobbly limbs struggled to let her stand.

"Casey! Are you okay?" Finnick's voice sounded toward her.

Within seconds, he'd burst through the open barn door with a black Labrador retriever at his heels. And for the first time in a decade, she looked up into the face of Inspector Ethan Finnick.

He'd had sandy blond hair that was lightening prematurely ten years ago. Now it was full gray and peppered with fresh snow. There were new lines on his handsome face.

Worry pooled in the depths of his eyes.

A snowmobile roared from behind the barn. Her attacker was escaping.

"Are you okay?" Finnick asked.

"I—I think so…"

Her breathing was getting stronger and steadier by the moment, and nothing felt bruised or broken. Finnick crouched beside her and reached for her hand. She reached up toward him. His strong fingers held hers tightly and pulled her up to her feet. Despite the fact he was wearing gloves, she could feel warmth radiating through his palm into hers. She remembered a moment like it ten years ago, when they'd sat at her kitchen table talking and his fingers had suddenly grazed hers. They stood there in the barn for a moment, face-to-face, with his hand still holding hers, as if to make sure she was steady before letting go.

"Casey, who attacked you?"

"I—I don't know," she said. "A man…in a shepherd mask and robes…that he stole off my scarecrow."

"Where is he?" Finnick asked.

"Gone… He ran." She watched as Finnick whispered a prayer thanking God that she was safe, and Casey felt the warmth in her hand move up into her chest. "I thought I saw someone when I was up on the roof, and I dropped my phone. When I climbed down I couldn't see anyone, then he jumped me."

"Okay," he said, "give me a second."

He stepped back and placed a quick call to the island's police chief, Rupert Wiig, who seemed to know exactly who Finnick was, and who she remembered he'd worked with before. She listened as Finnick relayed what she'd told him about her attacker.

The elderly black Labrador poked his head out from behind Finnick's legs. The dog's soft, black snout butted against her hand. He was Jackson's partner, Nippy, she remembered. She ran her fingers over his silky ears, brushing the snow from his fur. Nippy licked her fingers and his tail thumped on the wooden floor.

Finnick stepped away and exchanged a few more words with Wiig that she couldn't hear. Then he ended the call and turned back.

"Nippy remembers you," Finnick said.

There was an odd tone to his voice that she couldn't quite place.

"Wiig said he'd get his team looking out for the man who attacked you," he went on. "I told him I'd take your statement and relay any pertinent information to him. I'm afraid my van crashed on your lawn and the windshield is shattered. Also, I should tell you that a young woman ran out in front of my van and I had to swerve to avoid her. I don't know where she is now or if she's okay. So, I gave her description to the chief as well and he said he'd have people looking for her too."

Casey looked past him at the dark and blowing snow.

"I know it doesn't look like it, but there are houses five minutes' walk in all directions," Casey said. "And the center of town is twenty minutes on foot. She won't have to walk long for help. Thankfully, we have a really good neighborhood watch, organized by my big sister, Eileen."

The same sister who'd told her to take the creepy costume off the scarecrow. She fished her cell phone from her pocket, pulled up a text to her sister and handed it to him.

"Here, input all the details," she said, "and in a flash, Eileen will have every person on the island looking out for her. What did she look like?"

"Young, with long hair, and scared," Finnick said, as he typed. "She was holding something. It might've been a baby, but I can't be sure."

"A baby?" Casey repeated.

"I'm afraid so."

The text swooshed away from her phone and within a second, it pinged again as Eileen sent out an all-island alert about the woman.

He handed the phone back. "That's a handy neighborhood-watch thing to have."

"Eileen set it up after Stella and Tim vanished," Casey said. "I know everyone thinks that Tim killed Stella and then vanished, but—"

The piercing and panicked sound of a baby's cry rose suddenly on the wind.

Casey's heart lurched. Was this the baby Finnick had seen?

But even as she was about to ask, it was like something instantly snapped inside Finnick. Immediately, he turned without hesitation and sprinted through the snow toward the sound, even while her brain was still scrambling to process what was happening. Nippy ran after him and so did she.

Lord, help us find and save the child!

The plaintive cries seemed to be coming from the center of her nativity scene.

Then she saw the baby.

A real, live infant, no more than a month or two old, was lying in the manger, in between the figures of Mary and Joseph, with a note pinned to its chest.

SAVE ME.

TWO

Finnick whipped off his thick winter coat. Immediately, he felt the cold and wet weather smack his body. But he gritted his teeth and ignored it. If it was this bad for him, he couldn't imagine how bad it was for the tiny child. Thankfully, the kid was still bellowing.

Keep fighting. Stay strong. Stay alive. I've got you.

Carefully, he picked the child up, swaddled the infant in his coat and clutched the bundle to him. The baby snuggled against him as if craving Finnick's warmth. Something fluttered in his chest.

Then he glanced up. Casey and Nippy were by his side.

"Whose baby is this?" he asked.

Worry pooled in Casey's eyes. "I've got no idea."

"We need to get this kid inside. Now."

Casey didn't even answer. She just turned and ran toward the house. Finnick raced after her and Nippy stuck close to his side as if to help protect the child. They all arrived at the front door at once. Casey flung it open and then stepped back so Finnick could rush in first. The living room was just like he remembered, with a well-worn but comfortable couch and two chairs, an old steamer trunk as a coffee table, a kitchen to his right and a hallway straight ahead. Despite the abundance of Christmas decorations outside, there wasn't so much as a sprig of holly inside. Casey didn't even have a Christmas tree. Or any presents.

A fire smoldered in the fireplace. He knelt down in front of it and carefully laid the squalling baby down on a rug. Gently he unzipped the child's snowsuit, while Casey and Nippy hovered over him. It was soaked through, as was the white onesie underneath.

"Hang on." Casey turned, dashed down the hallway and disappeared through the door of what, if he remembered right, was her spare bedroom. An instant later she was back with a huge armful of red, yellow, blue and green onesies. They tumbled from her hands onto the floor beside him. His head shook. There must've been every size from preemie to toddler.

"How do you have—" he started.

But he stopped when he realized she'd already turned and dashed down the hall again, only to return with diapers, wipes and blankets. Casey vanished down the hall a third time. Nippy stood between the baby and the doorway. The dog's head was bowed in worry and his tail waved protectively. Gingerly, Finnick eased the child out of the wet clothes, checked the vitals as best he could and gently massaged the baby's tiny arms and legs with his fingertips to bring circulation back.

Strong heartbeat. Good breathing. No obvious injuries.

Thank You, God.

Then Casey was back, lugging a bassinet full of baby blankets over one arm and a folded wooden stand for it over the other.

"The tall cupboard in the kitchen has a few cans of formula and there are two bottles on the shelf above the counter," she said. "Sadly, only enough to get us through the first twenty-four hours. But at least it's something."

But why do you have all this baby gear on hand?

There'd been nothing about her having children in any of the research into Casey that his team had done. The question burned at the front of Finnick's mind. But it froze on his tongue as he saw the ache of sadness that pooled in Casey's eyes as she looked down at the child. Her chin quivered. And Finnick's instincts told him that whatever the answer to his question was, it was a tragic one.

Lord, whatever Casey's feeling right now, please hold her in Your hands. I need her to be strong right now. I can't do this alone.

"I'll get the formula," he said, quickly. "You get the baby changed. Thankfully, the kid is strong and healthy."

What looked like a silent prayer of thanksgiving crossed her lips, and tears filled her eyes. Casey nodded, set the bassinet down and knelt beside the child.

"Don't worry, Honey Bun," she murmured to the child softly. "You're safe now."

Finnick stood slowly and watched as she tenderly eased the infant onto a changing mat. He added an extra log to the fire, then turned and walked into the kitchen. Nippy, he noticed, stayed at his post by the baby's side. As he opened the cupboard, he found just three plates, two bowls and half a dozen cups...and an entire box of brand-new bottles and a bottle warmer that had clearly never been used.

The baby's cries finally stilled, and a sweet and gentle hush came from the other room.

When he emerged from the kitchen, he found Casey sitting on the chair closest to the fire, with the baby nestled in her arms.

"He's a boy," she said, softly. Casey looked up at him and her dazzling hazel eyes seemed to shine in the firelight. The child's own blue-eyed gaze also looked up at Finnick, curiously. "I'm guessing he's about six weeks old."

Finnick opened his mouth to speak, only to feel some unexpected emotion block his throat. So instead, he just handed her the bottle in silence and busied himself with setting up the bassinet and stand. Then he cleared his throat.

"Also, my sister texted to let me know the woman you nearly hit with your van has been found, safe and sound," Casey said. "She was seen getting into a white van at a gas station about ten minutes' walk from here and leaving the island."

"And leaving her baby behind," Finnick said. "The note pinned to his snowsuit said 'save me.' Why does this child need saving and who does he need saving from?"

To his surprise, thick tears welled suddenly in Casey's hazel eyes, slipping from the edges of her beautiful lashes. Finnick found himself dropping down to the floor and kneeling beside her chair.

"Hey," he said softly. "It's okay."

His fingers brushed her arm. But she stiffened under his touch. She shook her head and he pulled back.

"I didn't tell you everything that happened in the barn," Casey said. "I meant to, but there was so much happening at once—"

"Hey, it's okay," Finnick cut her off. "Don't beat yourself up for what you didn't say. Just tell me what I need to know now."

A look of relief flashed across her face, as if she'd been expecting him to berate her. While he wasn't exactly sure what to make of that, he mentally filed it away for later.

Casey ran her free hand over her face. Then her eyes met his, clear and direct.

"The man in the mask said, 'Where is he?'" she murmured slowly, as if trying to remember the exact words. "'Tell me where he is. Or I'll find him and kill you both.'"

He sucked in a painful breath.

"And you think he meant the baby?" Finnick asked.

"I don't know," she said. "I thought he meant Tim and that he was just another conspiracy theorist here to harass me."

He looked from her heart-shaped face down to the tiny bundle in her arms.

Lord, please give me the strength, power and wisdom that I need to protect them with my life.

"I had absolutely no idea he might've been talking about this baby," Casey added. "Like I said, a lot of people have written to me or called me with their crackpot theories about what happened to Tim and Stella."

Nippy sighed loudly, and even though Finnick logically knew it had everything to do with the warmth of the fire and nothing to do with the conversation that the humans were having, he felt the sigh with every fiber of his being.

"Stuff like *this* is why the Cold Case Task Force is so important," Finnick said. His voice was louder and more emphatic than he intended, and though the baby didn't stir, he could almost feel it reverberate through the room. "You've gotten used to being harassed. Nobody should have to get accustomed to that. And if we solve this case—"

He stopped and caught himself, feeling a stronger determination than he'd ever felt before move through him.

"—*when* we solve this case," he corrected himself, "then there won't be the same uncertainty hanging over what happened before." He sighed. "Look, I think it's a really normal and human thing to want answers when something bad and confusing happens." Like, he guessed, having a husband drive off with a co-worker and never be seen again. "But you've got to trust me that all I want to do is figure out what really happened to Tim and to Stella."

"Tim didn't kill Stella," Casey said. "I don't know where he is, where he went the day he disappeared or what happened to him. But I know he's dead."

"I hear you," Finnick said, "and if you're right and he's dead, I promise I'll do everything in my power to prove it."

Lord, I don't think I've ever wished that anyone was dead before. And I don't have it in me to hope for that now. So, I just pray that You help me find the truth. Wherever it leads.

"Okay," he asked her again, "so you have no idea who this baby is, where he's from or why someone left him in your manger?"

"None at all," Casey said. Her eyes locked on the child who was gulping down the bottle.

"I believe you," he said. And he did.

"Manitoulin Island isn't that big," Casey went on. "There's only one high school and a handful of churches. Juniper Cove itself has a population of six hundred and eight." Six hundred and ten, Finnick thought, counting himself and the infant. "Everyone knows everybody else's business on an island like this. I'm not saying I've met everybody, but you tend to hear when somebody's having a baby and I can't think of anyone who had a child in the past three months."

Finnick sighed and ran his hand over the back of his neck.

"We're going to have to call Child Protective Services," he said.

"The number is posted next to the phone in the kitchen," Casey said, "along with the extension of the social worker I've been working with. The closest office is on the mainland and it normally takes them a little over an hour to get here, when the weather's good."

"And you know this, how?" Finnick asked.

For that matter, he was still curious why she had a mountain of new baby clothes.

"They've got my home on file for emergency foster care," Casey said.

"You're a foster mother," Finnick said, slowly. A fact that had been missing from his briefing. "Do people know this about you? And are you the only one in Juniper Cove?"

"Yes to both," Casey said. "I'm the only safe location listed as an emergency place to drop off a foundling on the island."

"So, it's possible this woman was desperate," Finnick said, "and decided to take the baby somewhere she knew he would be safe. Have you ever had a child placed with you full-time?"

"Not yet," Casey said. "I've been qualified for three years. But each time one has come up, I've failed to pass the final background check. I think because someone in town who holds a grudge against me for what they think Tim did has been lodging anonymous complaints against me."

Her tone was light as she said the words, but still they hit him like a punch in the gut.

"I'm so sorry," Finnick said.

"It's fine," Casey said. "It just means going through a fresh batch of questioning and background checks. Every time I pass and get back on the list. But by the time it's all cleared up, the child who was supposed to be placed with me has ended up with another family."

She smiled sadly. Her gaze was still locked on the baby in her arms.

The tiny boy had finished his bottle. His eyelids closed and his little nose was scrunched in what seemed like sleep.

"Looks like he's dozed off," Finnick said.

"I think so too," Casey said. She shifted him deeper into the crook of her arms and dropped the bottle beside her on the chair. "Poor thing must be exhausted. Normally, the protocol for a foundling is to take them to the closest police station, and from there, CPS will place them in a foster home. I can't just keep him here without first going through the proper custodial steps. But considering the storm and the fact the closest police station on the island will still probably take us almost an hour to get to, hopefully they'll agree to release him into our care, what with my being cleared as a foster parent and you being a cop and all."

Our care. Jointly. As in hers and his together.

Casey looked from the sleeping baby to Finnick and shrugged slightly.

"Do you mind calling CPS?" she asked, with a small laugh. "I should, but I don't want to wake him up."

Finnick felt himself grin.

"Yeah," he said, "no problem."

"You'll also find the number for the island mechanic and the one on the mainland by the phone, so you can get someone out to fix your windshield," she added. "The island one is closed over the holidays, so you'll have to call the mainland shop."

Nippy raised his head as Finnick passed, but when the inspector didn't signal him to join, Nippy sighed and laid his head back down on his paws. Finnick felt his grin tighten in determination. If the Child Protective Services rep did express any concern about leaving the baby in Casey's care, Finnick would be all too happy to assure them that he was certain, from everything he'd seen, he had absolutely no doubt that Casey would take excellent care of the child.

Finnick added the fact that someone had apparently wrecked her dream of being a parent by lodging anonymous complaints against her to the mental file he was compiling on Casey.

Who would do such a thing? Was it really someone with a grudge—holding Casey accountable for her husband's crimes? Or did some of the locals think Casey was involved in what happened to Stella?

He placed the call to Child Protective Services on the kind of old-fashioned landline he hadn't used himself in years. He ended up on hold longer than he liked, but when he finally got through to a live person, gave his name and badge identification and explained the situation, it turned out Casey's prediction about the child being released into their joint care had been absolutely right. In fact, he had the impression the rep would've still preferred that Finnick and Casey take him to the closest mainland station, to go through the regular steps, if it hadn't been for the storm. Instead, Child Protective Services would be sending a representative out in the morning to take the baby into their care. They were expecting the rep to arrive between ten and eleven. Until then, he was released into Finnick and Casey's care as their joint responsibility.

He then reached the mainland mechanic, who said he was facing a long backlog of emergency repairs but would have someone out to fix his windshield by lunch tomorrow.

All right. So until then, the cop and the witness would be raising a child together in a winter storm.

He placed a quick call to Jackson's cell phone, got his voicemail and left a message saying that he and Nippy were fine, but he'd been in a minor fender bender so was spending the night on the island.

Filling Jackson and Gemma in on Casey and the baby could wait until they were actually talking on the phone. In fact, he should probably arrange a full team briefing.

He walked back into the living room

to find Casey curled up on the chair with her feet tucked up beside her, and the baby still asleep in her arms. Nippy was stretched out in front of the fire. The old dog seemed to be sleeping too. Casey met Finnick's eyes silently, and for the first time since he'd crashed onto her property, he watched as a tired but genuine smile crossed her lips. Heat rose to the back of his neck. He broke her gaze and busied himself with picking up the baby's wet clothes off the floor.

"You were right about CPS," he said, keeping his voice low so as not to wake the sleeping child. "They've released him into our joint care until a rep can get here from the mainland tomorrow. You were right about the mechanic too. I decided not to tell him I'm a cop, mostly because I'm not certain I want people in this town knowing there's an investigator here looking into Tim and Stella's disappearance yet. Sometimes, the longer we can keep the lid on what we're doing, the easier it is to get the information we need. So, for now, if anyone asks, I'd appreciate it if you tell them that my name's Ethan, I'm a friend of yours and I'm buying a box of your soaps and candles as last-minute gifts for a Christmas Eve dinner I've somehow gotten roped into. Which is true, actually."

Despite the warmth of the house, the baby's clothes were cold to the touch and the note that had been pinned to the baby's chest was so soaked it fell apart in his hands.

"Sadly, we're not going to be getting any DNA or fingerprints off of any of this," he went on. "And considering the storm, I doubt we're going to find any footprints."

He glanced out the window. Already their own tracks from the manger to the house were being erased. He turned his attention back to the baby's clothes. There was a smudge of blue ink on the label of his onesie. Finnick held it up and squinted.

"Joey," he read. "Apparently, our little

visitor has a name. Does the name Joey mean anything to you?"

The question was light as it crossed his lips. But then he glanced at Casey and watched as the color drained from her face.

Immediately, he sat down across from her on the metal trunk that served as a coffee table.

"What's wrong?" he asked. "Do you know who this baby is?"

Their knees were so close they were almost touching, and as he looked down he couldn't help but notice that her legs were shaking. So were her arms.

"No," she said. "I don't know. Maybe."

Quickly, she stood, crossed over to the bassinet and set Joey down amid the soft blankets.

Then she turned and looked at Finnick. Her mouth opened and then closed again, as if she was afraid of the words that were about to cross her lips. He watched as she whispered a prayer for wisdom.

"Hey, it's okay," he said, softly. "Whatever it is, you can tell me."

"I get a lot of unbelievable letters from people claiming to know the truth about what happened to Tim and Stella," she said, her voice barely rising above a whisper. "I don't take them seriously, but…" She trailed off. Her gaze looked past him to the sleeping child. "I recently got a letter from a woman named Ally, claiming to have given birth to a baby named Joey." Then her hazel eyes finally met Finnick's. Fear, doubt and determination all battled in their green-and-brown depths. "Ally wrote that Tim is still alive, and that Joey is his son."

"Joey is Tim's son?" Finnick repeated. The detective shot to his feet and began to pace. "You're telling me you got credible information that Tim Thompson, your former husband, might still be alive and have a son, and this is the first I'm hearing of it?"

Casey felt her head shake. At the end of the day, Finnick wasn't there to be her friend. No matter how good he seemed at listening, or how sweet his dog was. He was a cop, and he always would be.

Lord, I don't even know what to pray for right now, I just know I need Your help.

And so does Joey.

"It's not like you're making it sound," Casey said. Her arms crossed and although her voice was low, she packed every bit as much feeling into it as if she'd been on the verge of yelling. "I told you and your colleague, I've gotten hundreds of letters from people trying to scam, threaten or blackmail me."

She swept everything off the steamer trunk that served as her coffee table onto her couch. Books, mugs and unused baby clothes tumbled onto the cushions. Then she yanked the lid open and gestured for him to look.

Finnick stepped forward and glanced inside. Six topless boxes formed a makeshift filing system. So far, she'd filled five and a half of them, with hundreds of letters, each one of them in its own transparent plastic sleeve. Finnick frowned and sighed. But he didn't look surprised.

"Don't worry," she said. "I always wear gloves when I open them and slide them into a plastic sleeve immediately, in case some cop ever wants to see them."

"You might've done more work to solve this case than the original investigator who was assigned to it," Finnick muttered. "Not that I worked the case beyond the search Nippy and I did of your property. But we have his files and they're definitely lacking. Can I take that with me?"

"You can take all of it if you want," Casey said, "if it'll help you figure out what happened to Tim and Stella. But these aren't leads. They're letters from kooks trying to get money from me. Trust me, anything that contained anything resembling an actionable fact was turned over to police immediately. As for the rest, years ago, I dutifully reported each and every one to the police. People would claim they had seen him alive, knew who killed him or could prove his innocence— for a price. Each time my heart would be filled with all this foolish hope and I'd run to the police with it. Until eventually, an officer told me that sending letters wasn't a crime, unless they contained a clearly stated threat of violence, and that if police chased down every letter-writing nutjob in Canada, they wouldn't have time to go after real criminals."

Finnick's frown deepened and his brows knit.

"Well, whichever cop said that, it was 60 percent untrue," he said. "Depending on the volume of letters sent by any one individual, this could most definitely count as criminal harassment. But it is a hard case to make stick, and all too often results in a warning the first instance. So, the fact that you've been keeping track of them is probably the best thing you could do." He shook his head as he scanned the trunk. "I'm going to take a picture of this for my team. So they can see what some of our cold case victims might be dealing with and be understanding of that."

She felt oddly comforted that Finnick had just called her a victim.

"You got the baby Joey letter?" he asked.

"Absolutely." She was already scanning for it. A moment later, she pulled it from the trunk and handed it to him.

"This isn't even the first letter I received from someone claiming to have Tim's child," she said. "I've probably had over a hundred about secret babies alone. Not to mention all the other outlandish claims." That was the reason she'd filed Ally's letter away without thought. But now they'd actually found a baby named Joey...

Finnick pulled it gently from her hands, took it by the very edges and scanned it for a moment. Then he read it out loud. "'Hi Casey, You don't know me. But my name is Ally, I'm twenty years old and

I've been romantically involved with your husband, Tim Thompson, on and off for months. I just gave birth to Tim's son. His name is Joey. Send me twenty thousand dollars or I'll sell my story to the media. Ally.'"

Finnick turned the paper over as if hoping to find something more written on the back. Then he blew out a breath and ran his hand over the back of his neck.

"Wow," he said. "Not much to go on and she was trying to blackmail you. I can see why you didn't rush to the police with this one."

He sat down on the far end of the couch, away from all the stuff that had once been on her coffee table. She hesitated, then sat down on the opposite end, letting all the mugs, books and random items pool between them.

"Or think somebody was going to drop a baby off outside my house," Casey said, "with a note begging me to save him."

The question Finnick had asked earlier flickered in her mind.

Why does this child need saving and who does he need saving from?

"We can't assume that this baby is the same Joey from the letter," Finnick said. "I mean, it would be a pretty big coincidence if this Joey and the Joey in the letter aren't connected. But we can't just guess at it." He shook his head. "I hate to ask you this," he said, "but how can you be so certain that Tim's dead?"

Casey squeezed her eyes closed so tightly she felt tears building under the edges of her eyelids.

"Because I didn't marry an evil monster," she said. Her eyes opened and she could feel the tears now clinging to her lashes and hoped they wouldn't fall. "I'm sure you've heard that kind of thing over and over again, from people who can't admit their loved ones are criminals. But Tim was a real-life guy with a personality and faults, not the stereotype people want to make him out to be."

"Then, what was he like?"

"A goofball," Casey said. "A lovable, easygoing guy who'd spend twenty minutes chatting up elderly customers and would give people the shirt off his back."

There'd been something so safe and comfortable about being around Tim. His arms had felt like home. And his cheerful spontaneity had seemed like the perfect fit for a woman like her who'd felt perpetually stressed and who overplanned everything.

"Don't get me wrong," she went on, "I'm not saying he was perfect. He lent money generously, even when we couldn't afford it. He picked up hitchhikers and would be two hours late for dinner because someone he barely knew asked him to help move a couch."

And sometimes, despite having a good heart, Tim had made her feel like the least important person in his life. Because he'd been too busy chasing after everybody else's needs—whether they truly needed him or not—and he was never there to just hold her hand or sit on the couch together.

"He let people take advantage of him," Casey added.

"And how did that make you feel?" Finnick asked.

"Resentful," Casey admitted. "Then guilty for feeling that way. Because I knew he was a good guy who loved me and his heart was always in the right place."

"So, your theory of the case is that it was a random act of violence?" Finnick asked.

"I don't know," Casey said. "Maybe. I can't imagine anyone wanting to hurt Tim. All I can think is that Stella was in some kind of trouble, Tim leaped in to help her and he got caught up in whatever was going on. Wrong place at the wrong time, kind of thing. For all I know, it was a spur-of-the-moment decision on his part to take her wherever they were going."

"Can you think of anyone who'd have wanted to hurt Stella?"

Casey shrugged. "She was engaged to Drew Thatcher," she said. "But they seemed happy. Stella always seemed kind of withdrawn to me, and Drew was—well, he still is—a really outgoing, charming guy. Plus, he was at work and had an alibi."

She ran both her fingers through her hair.

"I wish people had looked harder at Patrick Craft," she added.

"Who's he?"

"Back then?" she asked. "He was Drew's best friend and the last person to see Stella and Tim together. He had a baby with his girlfriend, and she left him shortly after Stella and Tim vanished, leaving him to raise the kid alone."

"And where is Patrick now?" Finnick asked.

"Still on the island," Casey said. "He's the owner of Craft and Son Construction, which he inherited from his father. He's also the chief of our voluntary firefighters. I know you didn't get that good a look at my garage, but my soap-and-candle workshop is in the back and there's a loft bedroom in the rafters. He designed and built that. Did a similar one at my sister's house for my nephew. It may seem odd to a non-islander, but in a place this small, you can't afford not to get along with someone."

"And why do you wish police had dug deeper into him?" Finnick asked.

"Because I know Tim is innocent," she said, "and it seemed awfully convenient that Patrick just happened to see them leave the island together. I don't know, I just get a weird and unsettling feeling whenever I see him. He never really meets my eye. It's like he knows something he's not telling me."

Then again, going over a decade without answers had given her a lot of time to try to come up with alternative explanations for what might've happened. For all she knew, her suspicion of Patrick was no different than other people's suspicion of her.

Finnick nodded. "What happened to his kid?"

"Patrick's still a single dad. His son's name is Tristan and he's twelve now."

Finnick didn't answer. Instead, he went over to the fireplace, added a fresh log and then moved the wood around slowly with a poker, as if trying to get the positioning just right. Everything about Tim had been fast. The way he talked, the pace he walked, the speed at which he leaped into things without thinking, even the way he waved his hands around to punctuate whatever he was saying.

Finnick was the opposite of that.

Nippy had repositioned himself by the baby, with his snout on his paws, facing the child. For a long moment, silence fell around them, punctuated only by the crackling of the fire, the snow beating against the windows and the gentle wheezing sounds of Nippy's low snores and Joey's high-pitched ones mingling together.

"If you told me that Tim picked up a hitchhiker who'd murdered him and Stella, I'd believe you," Casey added, feeling the need to say something to fill the silence, "or that he'd been talked into driving her four hours roundtrip to Sudbury."

"But not that he was having an affair or that he killed anybody," Finnick said finally, still crouched by the fireplace. He hadn't made it sound like a question.

"No way."

Finnick turned and looked at her. The orange flames danced in his dark eyes.

"I believe you," he said. "At least, I believe you're telling me the truth as best you know it. But there might be things about Tim that you don't know. And if so, it's my job to find that out."

But what if the keen-eyed inspector and his gentle dog found out things she didn't want to know?

Finnick went back to the fire. And she wondered if he was strategically using the silence to give her time alone with her troubled thoughts. Or if Finnick was naturally just a quiet guy of few words at heart.

After a long moment, Casey turned toward the window and stared out at the night. She'd left the Christmas lights on and at least four inches of snow had fallen since Finnick had crashed his car.

She watched as snow moved past the windows in waves of white, punctuated by bursts of color from her changing Christmas lights.

"I noticed earlier that you've got a whole panorama of Christmas lights and displays outside your home," Finnick said. "But nothing inside. Not even a tree. Why is that?"

Until he spoke, she didn't realize that Finnick must've been following her gaze out the window.

"Juniper Cove is trying to win this competition to be named the Most Whimsical Christmas Village in Canada," Casey said. "My big sister, Eileen, is head of the committee. Her husband, David Wilks, is the pastor of the local church. This competition is a really big deal for Eileen—for everyone here, really—because the increase of tourists and publicity, not to mention the prize money, could make a huge difference to the town and the whole island. So it was important I do my part."

She glanced back at the window and her heart stopped as she saw a dark figure moving through the lights like a shadow. The man in the ski mask froze momentarily, standing there in the front yard, staring right at the windows as if trying to see who was inside. She covered her mouth to stop from screaming and waking the baby. But Nippy barked sharply, as if the dog had been suddenly jolted awake. She glanced at the Lab, who was now on his feet.

"What's wrong?" Finnick rose from his seat and crossed over to the window.

She looked out again, just in time to see the figure dash into the darkness and slip around the side of the house.

"There's someone outside. I think he was watching us."

THREE

The figure had vanished from her view.

"What did you see?" Finnick asked.

She looked up him and watched as his gaze darted from the window to his K-9 partner, to the baby who'd already begun settling, before finally resting back on Casey's face.

"A man in a winter ski mask was standing right there." She pointed to the empty spot where she'd seen him. "I thought he was looking right at me. Then he disappeared around the side of the house, toward the barn."

"I'm going to go check it out," he said. His words and tone were comforting, as if his focus was on trying to keep her calm. But he didn't manage to hide the worry and concern she saw in his dark eyes. "Hopefully, it's nothing to worry about and just some guy who was walking in the storm and stopped to take shelter. But you stay here, just in case."

He quickly crossed the floor toward Nippy, who was still on his feet, signaling to the retired K-9 as he went. Joey was still fussing softly but seemed to be drifting back off to sleep. Casey glanced outside again and saw nothing but lights and snow.

"Why did Nippy alert?" she asked.

"Oh, that wasn't a K-9 alert." Finnick shoved his feet into his boots. "Just a regular bark letting me know he heard something outside." He grabbed his coat and was still putting it on as he opened the door. "He only alerts to the smell of a dead body, and let's both hope you never witness that."

Finnick and Nippy ran outside and into the snow. He pulled the door closed behind him as they went, but the winter wind caught it and slammed it back open. She could vaguely hear Finnick calling back to her to close and lock it again, as he disappeared around the side of the house. But instead, she checked the sleeping child, then pulled the door only partially closed and stood in the doorway, looking out at the stormy night.

For a moment, she couldn't see anything but the usual lights of her Christmas display being tossed and pelted by the wind. The sound of Finnick shouting for someone to stop and Nippy's loud barks rose from the darkness.

Then she saw the man dash out from behind her house. His long legs were almost flailing as they churned up the deep snow, as if he was too frightened to remember how running worked. And even from behind, in the dark and in the winter clothes, she thought she recognized his shape or maybe just something about the way he was moving.

Cameron? Her nephew—Eileen's only child.

She'd always been incredibly fond of the twenty-two-year-old and was happy to see him whenever he sporadically dropped by. This was despite the fact she knew his general lack of responsibility tended to worry his parents to death.

No idea what he'd been thinking lurking around her property in a ski mask at night—if he'd even been thinking at all. But regardless for the reason for this foolishness, the consequences were about to catch up with him fast. In an instant, Finnick and Nippy were on his tail, chasing after him with such determination and speed it was as if they didn't even notice the snow.

"Cam!" Casey raised her hands to her mouth and shouted. "Cameron Joseph Wilks! Stop!"

The figure hesitated and glanced back, only to catch himself on one of the extension cords powering her lights. He lost his footing and tumbled headfirst into the snow. Yeah, it was her nephew all right. She pushed her feet into her boots without lacing them, yanked a blanket off the back of the chair and wrapped it around her shoulders, and then stepped out onto her front steps, just in time to see Finnick give Nippy a subtle and silent hand signal.

Nippy stopped running and stood in the snow, his tail suddenly wagging. Finnick stopped too, the pair maybe ten feet away from Cameron, and even from a side view she could see a warm and disarming smile cross Finnick's face.

Cameron pulled his ski mask up. His oval face was pale in the flickering Christmas lights. She hadn't seen him in almost a year, but he had that same expression in his eyes that somehow always looked hungry, despite the fact he'd packed on a couple of pounds while he'd been away at college.

"Auntie Casey!" he called as he scrambled to his feet. "I just dropped by to say hi and…and see if you had a pair of cross-country skis I could borrow. But when I saw you had company, I figured I'd just see if I could get them for myself."

Instinctively, she glanced at her watch. It was a quarter after ten.

"You could've just knocked and asked if you could check in the garage," Casey called back.

Finnick faced her and seemed to read her in an instant. She wondered what he'd seen there. But he was already turning back toward Cameron.

"I'm sorry, man." Finnick reached down and offered him a hand. The warm and disarming smile on Finnick's face seemed to radiate through his voice. "Nippy and I didn't mean to startle you."

Nippy waved his tail as if in agreement. Cameron took his hand and Finnick helped him to his feet.

"You doing okay?" Finnick asked Cameron. "All good? Nothing broken?"

"Yeah, I'm okay," Cameron said. He

brushed snow off his legs and jacket. "I didn't look where I was going and just slipped over an extension cord."

"There are a lot of them out here," Finnick conceded.

"When did you arrive on the island?" Casey called. "Your mom said you weren't coming home for Christmas. She said you were photographing a wedding."

And Eileen had sounded royally annoyed about it too.

"Got here a few hours ago," Cameron called back. "The wedding party canceled on me last minute and Mom really wanted me here to help take pictures of her Whimsical Christmas competition."

"Well, sorry for getting off on the wrong foot." Finnick chuckled. "My name's Ethan. I'm a friend of your aunt's and accidentally spun out when I was on my way to see her. Just got invited to a Christmas Eve shindig at a friend's house and figured Casey's candles and soaps would make some great gifts."

He patted Cameron gently on the shoulder. It was a reassuring, almost fatherly gesture. But Casey couldn't help but notice that he hadn't identified himself as a cop, and for the first time that she could remember, he'd introduced himself by just his first name. He told her he'd done the same with the mechanic.

Suddenly the eerie Creepy Shepherd mask flickered in the back of her mind again. Her breath stuttered as she remembered the feeling of his hands around her throat.

Lord, why am I hesitant to ask Cameron about that?

"Oh, you haven't seen the shepherd robe and mask my scarecrow was wearing around here anywhere, have you?" Casey asked, keeping her voice as light as she could. "Your mom gave me grief for it. Said it looked creepy. Well, somebody stole it earlier and jumped out at me wearing it. He scared me half to death.

Then he took off on a snowmobile before we could stop him."

She paused and waited for his answer. But Cameron just shook his head.

"No," he said. "But I'll be on the lookout. What happened to the van?"

"A woman ran out in front of me and my tires lost traction," Finnick said. "Your mom sent out a message about her to the neighborhood watch. She was your age or a little younger. Blond hair. Looked lost... You see her?"

"No." Cameron shook his head. "But Mom mentioned she'd been picked up by someone and left town."

He wasn't meeting her eyes or Finnick's. But where to start on what Cameron might be hiding?

"You want to come inside and warm up?" Casey asked. "I've got hot chocolate. We can catch up and then I can give you a ride home."

But her nephew was already shaking his head.

"Nah, I should get home before the snow gets worse," Cameron said. He took a step backward. "Plus at this rate, I'll be able to run home faster than you'll be able to shovel your vehicle out of the barn."

He wasn't wrong about that. A few more inches of snow had fallen since Finnick's arrival. She glanced up at the continuing snow and hoped the tow van would still be able to get through in the morning.

"Okay, well, I'll hopefully see you tomorrow!" Casey called.

Cameron had already turned and started back toward the road.

"Absolutely!" Cameron called. "Don't let my folks know that I was here. I think Mom wanted to tell you about it tomorrow."

He jogged back to the road, and for a moment Casey, Finnick and Nippy just stood and watched as her nephew disappeared from view. Then, even once he'd gone, Finnick stared into the empty space where the young man had vanished, before turning and starting back toward Casey and the house, with Nippy at his side.

Casey stepped back inside the house as he approached, thankful to see Joey was still asleep in his bassinet. She slid off her boots as Finnick and Nippy entered the house behind her.

"Well, that was suspicious," Finnick said dryly. "I can't remember the last time I saw a less convincing performance. Do you know what that was all about?"

"Not exactly." She shrugged the blanket off her shoulders and dropped it back over the chair. But Finnick stayed at the door and didn't take his coat off.

Okay, now how to explain her particular family dynamics to someone she barely knew?

"Cameron is a good kid," Casey said. "Well, I guess he's not really a kid anymore. But he's had some problems with money and responsibility. And I guess you could say that his mom—Eileen—is kind of controlling. But only because she thinks she knows the right way that everything should be done. Which is something she got from our mom."

"That must've been fun to grow up with," Finnick said.

Casey laughed. "As the younger sibling who never could do anything right? Yeah, it was a blast." She sat on the arm of a chair, her legs suddenly feeling too tired to hold her up anymore. "Anyway, she's probably got Cameron on some kind of curfew, and he snuck out to see me, then looked in the window, saw you were here and decided to leave in case you were someone who'd tell his mom. Which, granted, does not explain why he ran around toward the barn instead of just taking off."

Finnick ran his hand over the back of his neck.

"I have so many questions," he admitted. "Cameron is in his twenties, right?"

"Twenty-two," Casey said. "He was

born when I was fifteen. I was his first and only babysitter."

A smile crossed her lips. She'd liked Cameron from the start. For once, it had felt like there was someone in the family she could relate to. Somebody else who was too loud, too clumsy, awkward and never did anything Eileen or her mother thought was good enough.

"He always drops by to see me when he's in town," she added, "and never thinks to call and tell me he's coming."

"Do you think he'd ever steal from you?" Finnick pressed.

"I hope not," Casey said. "But I could see him borrowing something and forgetting to ever tell me. He's a bit irresponsible, not malicious."

Finnick's brows knit.

"And you said he had a curfew," he said. "At twenty-two."

"Well, Eileen would never call it that," Casey said. "That's my word for it. She probably just told him that it would 'mean a lot' to her and Cameron's father if he could 'see his way' to being in the house 'by ten, so that everyone gets a good night's sleep.' Or something like that."

She realized she was unconsciously mimicking her older sister.

"Any criminal history?" Finnick asked.

"I don't think so," Casey said. "He used to skip school and once got caught smoking behind the church when he was, like, thirteen. When he was eighteen somebody called his folks to let them know he'd been seen sitting inside the bar in the next town over. And they've never let him live it down. More recently he got into some financial trouble. I think he was gambling online and racked up some bills. Eileen is helping him out financially, so she tends to keep a pretty close eye on him when he's visiting. Don't get me wrong. They're really loving parents. They just hold him to a ridiculously high standard that he can never live up to."

And I've never had a hope of living up to Eileen's standards either.

Finnick nodded and there was something in his eyes that made her think he was hearing more in her words than she was saying.

"What did Eileen think of Tim?" he asked.

"That he wasn't good enough for me," Casey admitted, "and that I was making a mistake by marrying him. But once he disappeared, she was nothing but protective. Maybe even overprotective."

"And if she wanted to say 'I told you so,' she never came out and said it?" Finnick asked.

"Yeah, pretty much," Casey said. Joey was beginning to stir now. She'd have to make him another bottle and see about settling him in the crib in the spare room.

When she looked back at Finnick, his eyes were also on the child.

"Do you think Cameron had anything

to do with what happened here tonight?" he asked.

His voice was so calm it was almost emotionless. But that didn't stop her lungs from tightening in her chest.

"No," she said. "I don't think so. Why? What are you suggesting?"

"I'm not suggesting anything," Finnick said. "I'm keeping an open mind about everything. Maybe your nephew and your family have something to do with this child. Or with the 'Creepy Shepherd' who attacked you. Maybe they even have something to do with Tim and Stella's disappearance. Or maybe nothing at all. By my math, Cameron would've been about eleven when it happened."

He pushed the door back open again and a cold gust swept into the room, sending a shiver down her arms.

"I'm going to go get my stuff from my van, and then we're going to head to the barn," Finnick said. "You said we could use the loft?"

Casey nodded.

"It's actually pretty comfortable," she said, "and it's heated, because I can't let the ingredients I use to make my soaps and candles freeze. But I've got to warn you, some of the soaps and candles smell so sugary it's put me off sweet things like candy for good. There's a cot set up and sleeping bags. And it's got clear sightlines to the house. Or do you want me to set up a bed in the living room for you?"

Finnick hesitated for a moment. Then shook his head. "Thanks, but I need some privacy to check in with my team," he said. "Plus you said the cell signal was strongest out there. Just flash the house lights if you need us and we'll be right over."

"Will do," she said. "Hold on, I'll give you a set of keys so you're not locked out." She popped into the kitchen, pulled her spare key ring from her junk drawer and then came back. "The square one is for the barn's side door and the circular one is for the house."

"Thank you." He took the keys from her. His gloved fingers touched her bare ones for just an instant, and somehow, she felt an odd sort of warmth move through his hand into hers. His dark and handsome eyes met hers, and she had to bite the inside of her lip to stop herself from leaning closer and hugging him good-night. "Thanks again for letting me stay," he said. "Here's hoping everything will look a lot better and clearer in the morning. You sleep well."

"You too."

Then Finnick and Nippy disappeared out her front door and back into the snow. She shut it behind them, turned the lock and leaned back against the door, wondering why her heart was racing.

The barn was dark, but as Finnick and Nippy stepped inside, he felt a gentle warmth surround them, along with the smell of cinnamon, peppermint, lavender, clementines and a dozen other spicy, fruity and flowery scents he couldn't place. Casey had told him that the smell had put her off sweets. Now he could see how that could happen. He felt along the walls, found a light switch and turned it on. A gentle yellow glow filled the barn. It was large, with a garage for her van and tools in the front, and a workshop full of colorful wax and soap in the back. A narrow set of steps led up to the loft, with a railing on one side.

He started for it, but Nippy beat him to the stairs. Finnick glanced down at the black Lab.

"I'll carry the stuff up," Finnick said, "and then I'll come back to get you."

But already the dog was climbing up to the loft, slowly and stubbornly. Finnick snorted, tossed his bags higher over his shoulder and started after him, bracing his hand against the railing and his legs on the steps, in case the dog faltered and tumbled back down into him. The dog made it to the top, slowly but surely. Finnick dropped his bags and looked around. There was a cot against the wall, a cooler, a kettle, a lamp and more than enough blankets for an army. He spread one on the floor and Nippy promptly lay down on it.

Finnick sat on the edge of the cot and plugged his phone into an extension cord that poked out from underneath the bed. Within moments it sprung to life. He called Gemma, and she answered before it'd even rung once.

"Finnick, hi!" Gemma's voice came through the phone, sounding slightly worried but also like she was smiling. "We got your message. How are you? Are you still at Casey Thompson's?"

"I am and I'm good," Finnick said. "I'm staying on her farm. I'm sorry I kept you up."

"It's fine," Gemma said. "I don't normally go to bed until eleven. Do you want me to wake up Jackson? I doubt he's getting much sleep lately anyway. Between you and me, I expect Amy and Jackson to give up trying to plan a wedding and just elope any day now," Gemma went on. "He and Hudson are up here at the cottage almost every weekend, and now he's going to be with the team in Toronto, I'm guessing that'll play a role in where they buy a house."

Finnick prayed and silently thanked God yet again that Jackson would be joining them. While Finnick and Jackson hadn't always seen eye to eye, the K-9 officer and his search and rescue dog, Hudson, were one of the very best teams Finnick had ever had the privilege of working with. Finnick added an extra prayer of thanks for Gemma, Caleb and Lucas.

He filled Gemma in quickly about baby Joey, the man in the Creepy Shepherd mask who'd attacked Casey, the fact that a woman named Ally had sent a letter claiming that Tim was still alive and that Joey was his child, and the various other things that had happened and that he'd discovered since they'd last checked in.

"Got all that?" he asked, when he was done.

"I think so," Gemma said. He could hear the sound of her laptop keyboard clacking through the phone. "It's a lot. I have so many questions."

"I'm sure you do," Finnick said, "but I doubt I have many answers for you."

"So, where do we start?" Gemma asked.

Now, that was the right question. The sound of her keystrokes stopped, as if Gemma was waiting for further instruction. Finnick took a deep breath and blew it out, overwhelmed for a moment by the sheer size of the case and the number of potential leads. Then he decided to just lay everything out and trust his fledgling team.

"Contact Caleb and Lucas," Finnick said. "Make sure that they get a copy of the original police file on Tim and Stella's disappearances. I'm not going to assign specific tasks to each of you because it's a busy time of year, both for you all and the people you might be trying to contact to chase down leads."

Besides, by laying out the work and letting the team decide what each of them wanted to take on, it would give him an interesting perspective on them all and how they worked together.

"First priority is seeing if there are any missing person reports that match Joey or the woman I think I saw carrying him," Finnick said. "For now, I'm going to assume that she's his mother—Ally—who wrote to Casey, claiming that Tim was the baby's father. But we can't know any of that for certain."

"Got it," Gemma said. The sound of typing resumed.

"Then I want to pull together any recent suspicious activity we can find by anyone using the name Tim or Timothy Thompson," Finnick said, inwardly groaning as he did so at the realization of just how much work that would be. "Assume he's in Ontario, start at the island and move outward. But again, I don't want the team wasting their time investigating everyone in Ontario named Tim Thompson."

"I know," Gemma said, confidently. "Don't worry, I got it. We're not looking into everyone named Tim Thompson who bought a house, landed a job or got married. We're after people who used his name at some rundown motel whose IDs were dodgy, credit cards were fake, or stories didn't match up. If Tim Thompson's still alive, he's done a really good job of hiding under the radar so far. And the kind of people who have come across him aren't the type to run to the police about it."

Finnick exhaled and thanked God the private investigator had agreed to join his team. He suspected there'd be more than a few cold cases coming up where her civilian perspective would come in handy.

"But if Tim is still out there," Gemma

added, after a long pause, "why would he use his real name? Why not give Ally a fake name?"

"No clue," Finnick said. "Some criminals like bragging about who they are and what they've done, especially when they're trying to impress or intimidate someone."

Although nothing Casey had told him about Tim lined up with that.

"When I asked Casey who she thought police failed to look into properly she mentioned Patrick Craft, Drew's best friend, who was the last person to see Tim and Stella alive, and the only one who places them in Tim's car together. Also, see if you can find out who at Drew's work provided him with an alibi for when Tim and Stella vanished. Maybe there's something we can shake loose."

"Will do."

Then, instinctively, Finnick lowered his voice, as if Casey could somehow hear him all the way from her house.

"Also, I want someone to take a look into Casey's family," he added, "specifically her older sister, Eileen Wilks, who's married to the local pastor, David Wilks, and her son, Cameron, who's twenty-two."

Gemma's chair squeaked and he had the distinct impression that she'd just sat up straight. "Any special reason why?"

"Casey's nephew was skulking around the house earlier tonight," he said, "and when he was caught he made up some nonsense story about borrowing skis. Casey said he'd had some money problems and I wondered if he was trying to steal from her."

He didn't hear the sound of typing.

"And do you think this has something to do with the case?" Gemma asked.

Or was he asking his team to look into something entirely unrelated to the case because of his personal feelings, worry and general need to make sure Casey was okay?

"I don't know," he admitted. Both to

Gemma and to the question in his own mind. "So don't put a lot of time into it. Just a quick look to rule it out."

"Got it," Gemma said. "Anything else?"

"Isn't that enough?" Finnick asked. She laughed and so did he. "Okay, so today's the twenty-second," he went on, "which makes tomorrow the twenty-third. I'm expecting the mechanic from the mainland to be here around lunch, but I'm not going to leave until the social worker comes to pick up Joey, which I'm expecting to be sometime between ten and eleven. I'd like you to arrange a team meeting over the phone for eleven thirty. I'm not sure how good the connection is going to be here for a group call, but even if I get my windshield sorted and the van back on the road before noon, I won't be home until after six."

"You could come straight here tomorrow if you want," Gemma said, "and get here a day early."

"Thanks," Finnick said. "I appreciate

that. Really, I do. But I think I'll just come up Christmas Eve for dinner. It'll be good to see everyone together in person."

And despite that he'd prefer to return home first to regroup, there was no way he was going to miss his team's very first meal together.

The call ended soon afterward, and by then, Nippy was already snoring. Finnick found a light switch in the loft, which plunged the barn back into darkness again. Then lay back, looked through the window at the darkened farmhouse and prayed for Casey, for Joey and his mother, Ally, and that God would help him and his team discover what had really happened to Stella and Tim.

Help me, Lord, and guide me. This whole case feels like that kind of tangled mess Christmas lights are in when you pull them out of the box. I can't find the end or the beginning. I can't tell how many different strands to this there are and if

*they even fit together. I don't even know
where to start.*

Hopefully, his van would be fixed quickly,
and Joey would be taken into care, giving
him a few minutes to say goodbye to Casey
and tell her that he'd be in touch with anything new about the case.

An odd pang of something that almost
felt like sadness twinged in his chest at
the thought of saying goodbye to Casey.
It surprised him. It had only been a matter
of hours since he'd crashed into Casey's
life, and before then, he hadn't seen her in
a decade. How could he even be thinking
about missing her when he left?

FOUR

The first thing Finnick noticed when he awoke was the glare of the brightest sun he'd ever seen, shining through the windows and illuminating the wood around him like a spotlight. The second thing he noticed was that his nose was cold and all the comforting warmth the barn had been filled with the night before had somehow vanished in his sleep.

He glanced through the window at the farmhouse. Casey's silhouette was dancing around the kitchen with Joey in her arms. Although he couldn't hear her, something told him that she was singing.

Casey was such a beautiful, brave and incredible woman.

He added a final thought to the prayer

that had filled his heart when he fell asleep.

And, Lord, please help me finally find her the justice and happy ending to this tragedy that she deserves.

Instinctively, he reached for his phone, which told him both that it was a quarter after eight and that the cell phone service was down. Next, he flicked the light switch up and down. The power was down too, and judging from what he could see out his window, Casey didn't have any lights on in the house either.

Finnick stood slowly and stretched, feeling his old bones creak slowly to life. Then he heard Nippy whimper. The dog was standing at the top of the stairs, wagging his tail nervously.

"Don't even think about it," Finnick said. "It's too steep for your arthritis. Stay there and I'll help you."

He pondered his options for a moment, then just went with the easiest solution—picking the dog up and carrying him down slowly. Nippy sighed at the indignation but laid his head on Finnick's shoulder. When they reached the ground, Finnick set him on the ground and opened the barn door. A thick wall of snow tumbled toward them. At least another foot had fallen in the night, adding to the several feet already on the ground. The road had been erased under a perfect sheet of white that ran from field to field; his van was buried up to the hood and the nativity figures were wading in snow up to their knees. But the sky was cloudless and almost impossibly blue, and bright morning sun beat down on the snow.

Nippy bounded out the door with a joyous woof only to disappear into a cloud of powder and vanish under the white blanket. A second later the dog leaped out of the drifts and tumbled back into them, like he was a dolphin and the snow was his ocean. Finnick laughed. Man, he loved that dog. He grabbed a large shovel from inside the barn door and started to dig a path from the garage to the street.

He was just finishing up when he heard the roar of snowmobiles, and looked to see three of them slowly making their way toward him. The man on the front vehicle waved. Finnick waved back and then walked over as the machines came to a stop at the end of Casey's driveway. The drivers cut their engines and pulled their helmets off.

On the first sat a man in his thirties with a huge mop of curly hair sticking out from under his red pom-pom hat, wearing a giant, charming grin. The second held a tall, muscular man with an angular face, short hair, a bushy mustache and a more cautious smile. Behind him, on the back of his snowmobile, sat a boy who looked to be about twelve who was the spitting image of his father, but with a quicker smile and more relaxed shoulders. It wasn't until the young man on the third turned to face Finnick that he realized it was Cameron. Casey's nephew had a camera slung around his neck.

Nippy sniffed the air as the old dog followed Finnick toward the trio. For a moment, Finnick felt the faintest warning at the back of his spine telling him that the K-9 detected something on one of the men. Then Nippy's snout dipped back down and his tail started to wag.

Whatever he'd sensed, he'd either decided it wasn't important enough to tell Finnick about or it was too faint to trace.

"Good morning!" the tall man said. "We're just going door to door to make sure everyone's okay and see if anyone needs help, what with the power out, the roads closed and everything."

"Why, that's really nice of you," Finnick said. "I'm Ethan. This here is Nippy."

"Welcome to Juniper Cove," the tall man added. "I'm Patrick Craft, head of Craft and Son Construction, and also the fire chief of Juniper Cove's all-volunteer fire department."

"Well, that would explain the mustache," Finnick said.

Everyone laughed. The boy louder than the rest, as if he was the kind of kid who enjoyed good-natured joking at his dad's expense.

"Nice to meet you." Finnick turned to the young man sitting behind Patrick. "And this must be the son?"

The kid grinned. "I'm Tristan."

"Nice to meet you, Tristan."

"And I'm Drew Thatcher." The curly-haired man extended a gloved hand and Finnick shook it. "I own Thatcher Family Real Estate."

"'The perfect home for the perfect family,'" Finnick said, "I saw your sign on the way into town."

So, that would be Drew, Stella's ex-fiancé, and Patrick, the man who saw Tim and Stella leaving town together. Was it just a coincidence that the two of them, along with Cameron, were the designated welcome committee checking up on Casey? After all, it was a pretty small town. While she may have suspected the police didn't do a good enough job looking into Patrick years ago, she'd also hired him to renovate her garage.

"We just wanted to remind everyone that there's plenty of fuel in town for those wanting to top up their generators," Drew went on, "and the town's shops are all still open for anyone needing last-minute gifts or supplies. The roads should be open in about an hour and we're hoping the phones will be back up before too long as well."

"That's wonderful," Finnick said. At this rate, the social worker would still make her appointment to pick up Joey and he might manage to get his van fixed and back on the road by lunch.

"We're also distributing flyers for the Christmas events in town," Cameron added. He reached inside his jacket pocket, pulled out a yellow sheet on paper and handed it to Finnick, who took it and thanked him. "Mom says to tell everyone that they're all still running and nothing will be canceled due to the weather."

"That's quite the spin out you managed to do with your van last night," Patrick said, glancing at the vehicle. He shook his head. "You know the island mechanic is away over the holidays and the mainland guy is pretty backed up. It might be a few days until he can get to this. I'm still waiting for him to get snow tires on my delivery van. Apparently, he ran out of the right size and they're on backorder."

"Well, I've got a mechanic from the mainland coming to fix my van this morning," Finnick said.

"Not if he's planning to cross the bridge he's not," Drew said. "Bridge to the mainland is down. There was a major accident last night when a van crashed through the barrier. Who knows how long it will take to fix. For now, nobody is getting on or off this island."

Joey's big blue eyes looked around with curiosity as Casey carried him through the kitchen and stopped in front of the large front window. The tyke had been babbling and chattering nonsense at her nonstop, ever since she'd changed him that morning. Despite the traumatic events of the night before, and the fact he'd been separated from his mother, Joey was a happy little guy and something about him tugged at her heartstrings, just as hard as his tiny fist tugged at handfuls of her hair.

Then Casey felt the shiver of a warning brush her spine as she glanced out to where Finnick and Nippy stood, talking to the group of guys gathered in front of her house. Something was wrong. She couldn't even begin to guess what it was. But even with Finnick's back to her, she could somehow read it in the way his shoulders tightened and his back arched slightly, as if Drew, Patrick or Cameron had just told him something that Finnick didn't want to hear.

Or maybe it was something he'd been able to read in one of their faces.

Her arms tightened around the small baby, now bundled up in her arms. But she kept her tone cheerful and light.

"You and I are not going to worry about what's going on outside, Honey Bun," she said. "Because we're cozy and safe, and that's all that matters."

Ever since she'd first laid eyes on Joey, she'd felt the instinctual need to protect him.

But from what? She didn't know. Let alone whether it had anything to do with what had happened to Tim and Stella.

But, Lord, whatever it is. Please give me the strength I need to keep Joey safe.

She wrenched her eyes away from the window, despite how much everything inside her wanted to keep her gaze on the handsome inspector now talking to her nephew and the two men who were inexorably linked to the cold case that had ruined her life. Not to mention the impulse inside her to walk outside and hear what the men were saying.

Lord, help me trust in You. Help me trust Finnick and his team too. And also help me trust that the truth about what really happened to Tim and Stella will come out in Your time.

But, please, if it be Your will, make it soon.

What people didn't get about living in a small town was that, once you'd lived through a tragedy, it was impossible to ever escape the reminders of it. Stella's parents hadn't been islanders and didn't have any community roots. They'd retired and left the island in the year after their youngest child disappeared, to be closer to their other children and grandchildren. Last she'd heard, they'd never forgiven the police or the town for what had happened to Stella.

But everyone else involved in the strange disappearances had stayed.

After all, Patrick, whose eyewitness testimony had placed Stella in Tim's bright red car, had also been the man who'd renovated her garage, because hiring someone off-island would've sent tongues wagging. Drew had worked at the town's local ice cream and hamburger joint back then, alongside the woman he'd since married, and was raising three beautiful daughters with. Not to mention all of their families and friends attended the Juniper Cove Community Church, where Casey's brother-in-law officiated Sunday service. Or the fact Eileen ran the neighborhood watch and had a hand in every community event the island had ever held.

For all the songs that had been written about how hard it was to go through a romantic breakup in a small town where everyone knew everybody else's business, all those heartaches had nothing on what it was like to have a former husband who'd vanished and was suspected of murder.

A sudden jolt of pain yanked her head to the right, and her mind out of the past, as Joey managed to snag another fistful of her hair in his tiny grasp.

Casey laughed, feeling oddly thankful for the tug back into reality.

"Joey, be gentle please," she said to him, as she eased her blond hair out of his fingers and tucked the wisp behind her ear. "I'm making your breakfast now. It'll be ready in a moment."

Then she turned back to the stove, where oatmeal was bubbling in a pot on one burner, a bottle of formula was warming in a pan of water on a second and a kettle of water for coffee was boiling on a third. Thankfully, it was gas, which meant she still had heat to cook, despite the fact the power had gone out. The roads would be covered too, but she'd never known them to be closed for more than an hour or two.

Soon the oatmeal was ready, the bottle was warmed and the smell of fresh coffee filled the air. Thanks to the heavy winds and excessive winter wonderland outside, the case worker might arrive a little later than planned. But as a fellow northerner, Casey was sure that the social worker wouldn't let a bit of snow stop her entirely, even if she had tried to call ahead and found the phones down.

"Not that it wouldn't be nice to get a little more time with you," she told Joey.

He squealed and waved his hands in response, and Casey felt an unexpected lump form in her throat. She swallowed it back.

"Breakfast is ready, Honey," she said, playfully, keeping her voice light. "Now, your options are formula or coffee."

Footsteps creaked on the floorboards behind her. She turned and met Finnick's dark eyes. They were wide with surprise. His lips parted, and then closed again, as if she'd somehow knocked the words right out of his mouth.

But for a long moment, she didn't actually realize what she'd just said or done that had surprised him. Nippy stood by his knee, with his head bowed slightly and his tail wagging slowly as if he could tell his partner had been thrown by something, but the K-9 didn't know what. Neither did Casey.

Finnick recovered his voice first.

"I'll take the coffee, thanks," Finnick said, with a weak smile.

A hot flush moved across her cheeks.

Did the Inspector Ethan Finnick, Head of the Ontario Cold Case Task Force think she'd just playfully called him *Honey*?

"Oh, um, I'm sorry," she started, without having any idea how her sentence was going to end. "I... I..."

But before she could find her words, Joey let out a loud and frustrated cry. His tiny fists waved.

"He's hungry," she said and quickly passed the baby into Finnick's arms, even as he opened them to reach for him.

She turned back to the counter, plucked the warmed bottle of formula from the pot and let a couple of drips fall on the inside of her wrist to check the temperature. Then she turned back. "The snow might slow the social worker down a little bit," she added, "but I still want to get him fed, changed and ready."

"The bridge is shut down," Finnick said. "A major accident, and won't reopen for hours. Maybe not even until tomorrow or Christmas."

And tomorrow was Christmas Eve.

"You're kidding." She blinked.

"I wish I was," Finnick said and frowned. "Because I was really counting on getting my windshield in and getting off this island this afternoon. And you weren't kidding about the mechanic being slow. Apparently, Patrick's still waiting on snow tires for his delivery van, which is nuts considering the snow up here." Joey squawked loudly in protest. "I'll fill you in more in a second. Let's get the kid eating first."

He took the bottle from her outstretched hand, and his fingers brushed against hers. Finnick tucked Joey into the crook of his arm and repeated the same temperature test on his wrist that she had on hers.

"So, you really do investigate everything," she said.

"I wouldn't be much of an inspector if I didn't." He grinned almost sheepishly and gestured to the tiny drip of formula now running into his sleeve. "But truth is, I did that instinctively."

His comment had been light and so was hers. But internally she was reeling from everything he'd just told her.

The bridge to the mainland had been out of use before, especially during the summer when it swung up to let boats through. But it had never been shut for more than an hour. Let alone a day.

Just how long were Finnick and Joey going to be staying?

Finnick offered Joey the bottle, but despite how loudly he'd squawked for it just moments earlier, the baby's lips now stayed stubbornly closed.

"Come on, little man," Finnick said. "I know I'm not as sweet or nice smelling as Casey, but don't hold that against me."

He chuckled softly as Joey hesitated for another moment, then took the bottle and began wolfing it down, with loud and determined sucks.

"By the sound of things, it's a pretty big accident," Finnick told Casey. "A van jackknifed on the ice. It needs to be removed before they can fix the bridge. And then they'll have to worry about the lineup of people trying to get on and off the island."

Especially considering the bridge was so narrow, traffic could only go in one direction at a time.

"Internal island roads should be open in an hour or so," Finnick added. "It's just a matter of mobilizing snowplows."

"Thankfully the island has several of those," Casey said.

"They're also hopeful that electricity, cell phones and landlines will be fixed soon," Finnick said.

"Presuming none of the damage is so

serious they need a repair crew from the mainland, right?" Casey said.

"Exactly," Finnick said and frowned. "But for now, I'm stuck here."

Stuck on the island? Stuck with her? Or both.

Casey sighed, and Nippy walked over to her and butted his head against her leg, as if wanting to help. She reached down, ran her hand over the back of the dog's head and scratched behind his ears. His fur was wet from the snow.

"I'm sorry, pupper," she said. "I don't have any dog food. The best I can do is cut up some lunchmeat for you. Unless you like oatmeal."

"Actually, he likes root vegetables," Finnick said. "Carrots or squash are his favorites, if you have anything like that."

"I have some chunks of pumpkin in my freezer," Casey said, "fresh from my garden." She pulled them out and put some of the veggies in a pan to warm.

"Perfect," Finnick said. "Thankfully,

according to our visitors, most of the main stores in Juniper Cove are still open and running on backup generators. Plus there's an indoor Christmas market in the town hall. Apparently, all the Whimsical Christmas events are still on."

"There's a Christmas Eve nativity pageant scheduled for tomorrow with the island's children," she said, "followed by outdoor ice-skating. The volunteer firefighters turned a shallow part of the cove into a rink."

Casey grabbed a pad and pen off the counter and began writing a shopping list.

"I'm going to get some extra baby food in town," she said, "and of course dog food for Nippy."

"Do you have a generator?" Finnick asked.

"In the barn," Casey said, "but I'll need to get it hooked up to the house. Usually I just ride out blackouts with my fireplace and gas oven."

Because for the past ten years, she'd only

had herself. Casey hadn't had a man, his dog and a baby to worry about too. A mismatched and unexpected family of sorts, who were now cut off from the mainland and would be hunkering down together.

Casey spooned ladles of oatmeal into two bowls and set some warmed pumpkin in a third bowl on the floor. She then poured two cups of hot coffee while Finnick finished feeding the baby and burped him.

Next, she got a car seat and set it in the middle of her small kitchen table. Finnick placed Joey in there. Then Finnick, Casey and Nippy ate a simple, peaceful breakfast together while Joey sat in the middle, his wide eyes watching them all.

It was a quiet meal—but a soft, safe and comfortable kind of quiet. The kind filled with silent glances and simple smiles.

This was the place where Finnick had lived in her memory. Ten years ago, he'd been sitting across from her in the same chair at the same table. She'd been talking about Tim and started to cry. Partly it had been because she'd been sad and she missed him. But there were other feelings too, all muddled up together. She had been frustrated at the fact it had been almost a year with no answers, and angry at Tim for being the kind of guy who'd randomly leave the island without telling her. She'd been scared that she was now going to be alone for the rest of her life. Then, silently, Finnick's dark eyes had met hers. He had reached across the table for her hand and squeezed it, filling her with more comfort, understanding and strength than any hug she'd ever had. Over the years, as the memory had flickered across her mind, she'd tried to underplay the images and convince herself it had been meaningless, or even an accidental touch somehow.

Maybe because something about the memory was too powerful to let herself believe it was real.

But now, face-to-face with Finnick, sitting in the same places they'd been before, she knew without a doubt that Inspector

Ethan Finnick would never have taken her hand like that if he hadn't meant something by it. Even if it was just to let her know that he was sorry for what she'd been through and that she wasn't alone.

Twenty minutes later, breakfast was done, the dishes were tidied and the foursome was getting dressed in their winter gear to head out across the thick snow toward Juniper Cove.

Casey wore Joey close to her heart in a chest harness, which she then zipped up inside her puffy, oversize, white ski jacket so that only his little head—decked in a fuzzy green hat—stuck out the top. Joey could watch the world go by as they went.

To her amusement, Finnick dressed Nippy in a smart black-and-red-plaid jacket, which pretty closely matched Finnick's own faded plaid winter jacket. Then Nippy stood stoically and allowed Finnick to slide bright red doggie boots onto each of his paws.

"I know you don't like wearing them,

bud," Finnick said. "But we're both getting older and bundling up will help with
your arthritis."

They made their way down the narrow path that Finnick had dug from her
front door to the road. Then they tramped
down the road itself, following various
snowmobile tracks. The night before,
the snow had been blowing so heavily
they'd barely been able to see across the
street, let alone all the way down the hill
to Juniper Cove's Main Street. No wonder Finnick had been worried about how
far Joey's mother would have to walk to
find shelter. Now, in the bright morning
sun, they could clearly see the surrounding farmhouses, each wrapped in a vir-
tual spiderweb of unlit multicolored bulbs,
with lawns full of large dormant figures
of snowmen, reindeer and other animals
made out of lights, waiting to come to life
when the power came back.

Canada's Whimsical Christmas competition was supposed to be sending at

least one secret undercover judge to each community over the holidays—not that Casey imagined any undercover judges would be able to make it onto the island with the bridge closed. Although, along with decorating their houses, Eileen had specifically requested that everyone dress as Christmassy as possible. Which Casey had completely forgotten about until she started noticing just how many townspeople they greeted on their walk to town were decked out in hats with pom-poms and antlers, brightly patterned scarves and even some Christmas sweaters gamely pulled on overtop of their coats. Suddenly her own red hat and gloves, which had always helped put her in the Christmas spirit, felt downright grinchy.

As they approached the center of town, the sound of carolers rose to greet them from the live choir that stood on the steps of Juniper Cove's community center. They were dressed in their Dickensian best, including top hats, bonnets, flowing skirts and an abundance of ribbon. She spotted Cameron down the street taking pictures of the choir from a distance. He waved and then returned to shooting.

Garlands were wrapped around every lamppost, wreaths hung from every light, and it was like each and every shop had tried to outdo their neighbors with the sheer volume of stars, trees, snowflakes and holiday greetings that bedecked their windows.

As they drew closer to the town square, she heard Finnick suck in a breath.

"What's up?" she asked.

Finnick bent his head close to hers as if he was afraid the throngs of carolers and well-wishers would overhear him.

"I haven't attended a Christmas event in over twenty years," he admitted. "When I joined the force, my father was dead and my mom was in a retirement community and never minded if I came to visit her a day before or after the holidays. So I always volunteered to work so that those with families and kids could spend Christmas with their loved ones." He chuckled, softly. "Now it feels like two decades of Christmas celebrations have caught up with me and tried to trap me inside a giant snow globe."

Their footsteps grew closer to the carolers and now Casey could see her older sister leading the choir. Chestnut curls stuck out from under the brim of Eileen's bonnet and she wore green gloves that buttoned up to her elbows. When she spotted Casey, Eileen quickly brought "O Come All Ye Faithful" to a rousing end and then handed her baton to Drew's wife, Jessica. A soft-spoken woman, Jessica had had a well-known and hopeless crush on Drew for years before they were brought together by Stella's tragic disappearance. Jessica carefully tucked her sleeves into her own long gloves and took the baton.

Casey quickly pointed them out to Finnick as Eileen crossed the street toward them.

"That's my sister," she said. "The woman

who's just taken over for her is Drew's wife, Jessica, and the three blonde girls in the blue bonnets, in the front row, are their kids, Sophie, Lily and Molly."

"Why aren't you in the choir?" Finnick asked.

"Eileen says I've got a voice like nails-on-a-chalkboard—"

"Cassandra!" Eileen called before Casey could even finish the thought. "I'm so glad you could make it!" Her arms opened wide for a hug, then she hesitated as she saw the small bundle against Casey's chest. "Oh, you have a baby?"

"Yes, he was abandoned at my house last night," Casey said, "and I'm keeping him safe until the social worker can collect him. We think his name is Joey."

Eileen tutted affectionately and then sighed.

"No doubt left by the girl you texted me about," Eileen said. "I don't know what this world is coming to. Babies having babies, and then abandoning them! I blame the parents. David and I told Cameron that if we ever caught so much as a whiff of him getting involved in nonsense with the wrong type of girl, or going to parties or bars, we'd cut him off financially in a heartbeat."

She shook her head again, then turned to Finnick and smiled.

"I don't believe we've met." Eileen stretched out her hand toward him. "I'm Casey's big sister, Eileen. My husband is the pastor here in town and that's my son, Cameron, taking the pictures. He's studying photography in Toronto."

"Nice to meet you," Finnick said. He took her hand and shook it warmly. "My name's Ethan. This is Nippy, short for Nipissing. I was hoping to buy some last-minute Christmas gifts from your sister. Sadly, my van spun out on the ice and I busted my windshield."

Eileen's eyes widened, as if a light had suddenly dawned and it was flashing at her in warning.

"I'm so sorry to hear about your van," she said. "If you could please excuse me for a moment, I need to steal my little sister away for a few moments to discuss a Christmas thing."

"Of course," Finnick said.

To Casey's surprise, Eileen took hold of her arm and led her a few paces away down the sidewalk.

"How well do you know this man?" Eileen whispered, urgently.

"Not that well," Casey admitted. *He's a cop investigating Tim and Stella's disappearance, actually.* The words crossed her mind but stopped at her lips. After all, Finnick had asked her to keep that information under her hat for now. "I met him once, briefly, when he visited the island a long time ago. He crashed his van on my property last night during the storm and I let him stay in my barn until he could get it fixed."

"In your *barn*?" Eileen sounded horrified. "Casey! He could be an undercover judge! We have to get him set up in the Candy Cane Bed and Breakfast. They've got gingerbread muffins and peppermint coffee. Not to mention fresh, tree-patterned down quilts on all the beds."

Casey bit the inside of her lips to keep from laughing. She looked back at the street to where Finnick and Nippy were still watching the carolers.

"It's okay," Casey said. "Ethan is not a judge."

"Like he'd tell you the truth about that!" Eileen said. "The competition rules clearly state that incognito judges will be making undercover visits over the holidays to evaluate us on hospitality, ambience and overall expression of the Christmas spirit. Now, I'm sure whatever you did for him last night was as adequate as you could manage, but it's important that you encourage him to visit the town center to see everything Juniper Cove has to offer."

Joey cooed softly as if trying to get her attention. She wrapped her arms around him over the top of her jacket and pulled him closer to her.

Was it really the worst thing, if Eileen was convinced that Finnick was there to judge how Christmassy the town was? This Whimsical Christmas competition meant so much to her sister. Casey couldn't imagine how distressed she'd be if she knew a detective had shown up to investigate a cold case in the middle of it.

"That's not what I think," Casey said. "But you can talk to him for yourself."

After all, once Eileen had her mind made up it was almost impossible to change.

"You go on ahead into the Christmas market," Eileen said, "and I'll give him a quick tour of the town. I'll introduce him to everyone and make sure he gets to see the best side of Juniper Cove." Casey opened her mouth to respond, but before she could get a word in, Eileen was patting her arm. "I'm going to go tell Jessica to take over the choir. Don't worry, I'm sure everything will be fine."

Eileen hurried back across the street to the singers. Finnick sauntered over.

"What was that all about?" he asked.

"My sister thinks you might be an undercover judge, here to evaluate the Christmas competition."

Finnick snorted.

"She wants to give you a tour of the town while I'm in the indoor market," Casey added.

Finnick ran his hand over his jaw.

"That's not the worst idea," he said. "People will be a lot more eager to talk to me if they think I'm a judge."

Eileen was already walking back toward them. Finnick fixed his eyes on Casey's face.

"Are you going to be okay?" he asked.

"Yeah, the market's pretty awesome and half the town will be in there. Eileen also wants you to move into the bed-and-breakfast. She's impossible to say no to, which is why I never do," Casey said, with a self-conscious laugh.

"Well, I'll be the one saying no to her, not you," he said. "Stay safe and I'll meet you in the market when I'm done."

Finnick looked down at Joey and something softened behind his eyes as he ran his hand over the baby's back. Then, before they could talk any further, Eileen was there and enthusiastically offering to give Finnick the grand tour. Goodbyes were said, and then Eileen led Finnick and Nippy down the street.

As Casey watched them go, she felt an almost sour feeling begin to rise. Eileen had never taken her seriously. Or thought she did anything right.

Casey headed into the Christmas market. Immediately, she was surrounded by the warmth, sounds and smells of the holidays. She unzipped her coat so Joey wouldn't get overheated then moved through the stalls. She bought a quiche, a meat pie, soup and fresh bread for easy meals. Then she added a couple of sweet handmade outfits for Joey and some simple baby toys. On impulse, she also bought a soft green scarf for Finnick along with a matching dog scarf for Nippy.

Yet no matter how many beautiful stalls she visited and Christmas greetings she exchanged, the memories of how Eileen's thoughtless and critical words after Tim left filled her mind and wouldn't let her rest.

If only you'd paid more attention to your husband, Casey, maybe Tim wouldn't have left the island without telling you where he was going. Then we'd all know what happened to him and Stella.

And now, Casey was at risk of losing the farm that had been in Tim's family for four generations.

Suddenly the hall seemed to be getting hotter. The chattering around her seemed to grow louder. An emergency exit caught her eye to the right. She pushed through the door and found herself out in a narrow alley behind the community center.

Silence surrounded her. Cold air filled her lungs. Light snow fell down soft and gently around her. She zipped her coat back up around Joey and discovered the baby had fallen asleep. She cuddled him close as a sudden cry for help filled her heart.

Help me, Lord, I'm so overwhelmed.

Had she ever asked God to help her before? Except of course for desperate prayers when in an emergency. Casey wasn't sure. She'd spent countless hours beseeching God to help Tim, Stella, the police and all those touched by the cold case. But she couldn't remember if she'd ever specifically asked God to help *her*. Maybe she hadn't thought she deserved it?

Casey turned to go back inside, only to find the handle locked. She knocked, and when she got no response, she turned and walked through the quiet alley back toward the front of the building. The faint sound of carolers rose on the air.

Too late she heard the crunch of footsteps behind her. Then, before she could swing around, a strong hand clamped over her mouth. What felt like the muzzle of a gun pressed hard into the small of her back.

"Hello, sweet pea," a harsh and artificially deep male voice whispered in her ear. "I don't want to have to kill you. I'm just here for the kid."

FIVE

Panicked tears filled Casey's eyes and froze in her lashes, as the unseen menace behind her tightened his grip on her mouth. Her shopping bags fell from her hands. The muzzle of the gun dug painfully into the small of her back.

"Now you're going to take me straight to wherever you've got the kid," the man hissed, "and you're not going to do anything to stop me. Got it?"

And just like that a slight and fleeting hope crossed her heart.

He didn't realize she was carrying Joey, hidden safely inside her jacket, with only the top of his tiny head showing. The moment he realized Joey was there, he'd try to snatch the baby from her. Or maybe even kill them both. But for now, Casey had one tiny chance to get Joey to safety.

She had to get him to Finnick.

"Now, nod so I know that you've heard me," her attacker said.

She nodded slowly to show she was listening. Her hands crept up to the tiny baby strapped inside her coat, and she cradled him close to her chest, silently begging Joey to stay quiet. Slowly, she pulled up the zipper as far as she dared while still allowing him space to breathe. As long as Joey didn't make a sound, and her attacker didn't realize he was there, she still had hope of saving him.

Desperate prayers filled her heart.

Guide me, Lord. Help me save Joey's life. I cannot let this man lay a hand on him.

The man pushed her forward and they started walking slowly toward the back of the building. He was taking her to an even more isolated area. The sound of carolers began to fade. A window loomed ahead on the opposite building. But the blinds were down on the inside and there was no way to signal for help. She waited until they drew level, then risked a quick glance sideways, hoping to catch the reflection of the man holding them captive. For a fleeing moment, all she saw was her own terrified eyes looking back at her over a black leather glove. Then they took another step and there, in the glass, was the distorted reflection of the rubbery Creepy Shepherd mask and green robes she'd seen the day before.

His gloved hand moved from her mouth to her throat and squeezed just enough to send the fear of what he'd do if she didn't cooperate coursing through her. She opened her mouth, wanting to scream, but she could barely manage a whisper.

"Tell me where to find the child!" His unsettling voice filled her ear.

"Candy Cane—" she sucked in a pain-filled breath "—Bed and Breakfast."

The hand snapped back to her mouth.

He started leading her behind the buildings to the inn, taking a path where nobody would see her, until she could no longer hear the sound of the carolers singing or the hustle and bustle of the noise on the street. All she could hear was her own ragged breathing and their footsteps crunching in the snow. What would happen when they reached the bed-and-breakfast? Would he send her in alone to get the baby? What would happen if she tried to scream for help?

Would Finnick and Nippy even still be there?

Joey stirred softly, with a tiny whimper, like he couldn't decide whether or not to wake.

Please, stay quiet, Joey! Please stay asleep. If he realizes you're here I don't know if I'll be able to stop him from hurting you.

The Creepy Shepherd pushed her forward roughly, one step at a time. Casey could feel the desire to fight rising up inside her. She wanted to reel around and elbow him hard in the face, risking that he wouldn't be able to get a shot off that fast. But if she fought back, she'd be putting Joey in danger, and she couldn't do anything that would risk his life.

She had to stay calm and focused. She had to make it to Finnick.

Joey whimpered again, louder this time. Casey tried to cough to cover the sound.

Please, Joey! Just a few more moments!

But it was too late. Suddenly she felt the Creepy Shepherd's hands snap roughly to her shoulders and fling her around roughly to face him. Her foot slipped on the snowy ground and she fell back. Her hands shot out behind her, desperate to break her fall and protect the baby strapped to her chest.

A long, loud and plaintive wail rose from Joey's lungs as Casey felt her body hit the snow, shattering any lingering hope that she might be able to hide the child.

The Creepy Shepherd loomed over her. Angry, swear-laden words and syllables spilled incoherently from his lips. For a moment, he seemed too apoplectic at the realization she'd just fooled him to even form his vile threats into anything understandable. The gun shook violently in his hand as if he was too enraged to steady it. Then he dropped it somewhere in his billowing robes and lunged at her.

"Give him to me!" he shouted.

The Creepy Shepherd yanked the zipper down and grabbed at Joey, trying to pull him out of the carrier. Joey howled louder.

A yell ripped from Casey's lungs, so powerful it was like it'd come from somewhere deep inside her.

"You. Will. Not. Hurt. Him!"

She continued to scream for help, both in the hope that anyone might hear her and run to her rescue and also to God above. She fought back as hard as she could, desperately pushing the man's hands away before he could succeed in stealing Joey from her, and trying to rip off his mask.

But she was still down on the ground

and he was standing above her. The Creepy Shepherd grabbed for the child again and she could hear the Velcro on the carrier begin to rip. Her attacker was bigger than she was, she was short of breath and he still had a gun. It was only a matter of time before he overpowered her and took Joey.

Help me, Lord! Please! I need You now!

Suddenly she heard the faint sound of a dog barking. It was followed by the sound of a man's voice shouting.

Nippy and Finnick! They'd heard their cries and were coming to their rescue.

For a moment, the Creepy Shepherd hesitated, as if debating whether to just wait until they arrived and kill them all. Then he turned and dashed off between the buildings in a blur of green fabric.

Casey gasped a breath—*Thank You, God*—and tried to push her shaky legs to stand. Before she'd even made it up, she heard Finnick call her name and then felt his strong, hands reaching for her. She stumbled to her feet, but he still held on to her, as if knowing somehow that his grip was the only thing keeping her quivering legs from collapsing.

"Are you okay?" Finnick asked softly.

Casey opened her mouth to speak, but no words came out. Instead, she shook her head, and then found herself tumbling into his arms and starting to cry. Finnick held her gently, creating space for the whimpering child still strapped to her chest. Nippy pressed up against her legs, filling her with his warmth.

Why was Finnick holding her and comforting her? Why wasn't he chasing after her attacker? Why wasn't he letting her fall? Making sure that she was all right wasn't important, was it?

Why is he putting me first?

Questions cascaded through her mind. But she hadn't cried in front of anyone in years, let alone sobbed on a shoulder, and now that she'd started, it was like she couldn't stop. Joey's cries faded and the baby began to coo softly, as if comforted by the warmth of both Casey's and Finnick's arms around him. She glanced down to see his huge blue eyes looking up at her. Then Joey smiled.

She laughed through her sob, then slowly pulled back out of Finnick's arms.

"Are you okay?" he asked again. "What happened?"

She nodded and this time she was able to find her words.

"The Creepy Shepherd just tried to kidnap Joey."

Concern filled his dark eyes. "Same man as last night?"

"Yeah," she said. "Same disguise and deep, distorted voice."

Finnick let her go, and then reached down to run a gentle hand over Joey's back.

"Did he hurt you? Either of you?"

"No," Casey said. "I tried to lure him to the Candy Cane in the hopes of reaching you. Then when Joey started to cry, he tried to yank him out of the carrier. Thankfully, you heard us."

"Nippy heard you," Finnick said and finally broke his gaze on Joey to look down at his K-9 partner. "We were standing outside the bed-and-breakfast. His ears just perked, he woofed and started running. I took off after him, not even knowing what he was on about. I just mumbled something like, 'I'm sorry. Nippy says we've got to go.' Your sister and the other people I was talking to must have thought I'd lost my mind. I'm sure nobody could hear you. I couldn't even hear you for a while." He chuckled in amazement. "Nippy is a very good dog."

He ran his hand over the elderly animal's head. Nippy's snout rose happily, as if he could hear the pride in Finnick's voice.

"A decade ago, Nippy was cross-trained in search and rescue," Finnick went on. "But he wasn't quite as good at it as he was at tracking cadavers, and since there were already a lot of dogs in search and rescue, we decided to drop it. I guess he didn't forget. They only retired him due to his age, and some arthritis in his hips. You never want to risk having a dog on the case who's not up to the task."

Finnick closed his eyes and took a deep breath, and she wondered if he was praying. Casey shivered, as if her exhausted body had finally registered the cold. Finnick exhaled and opened his eyes again.

"Okay, I'm going to call this in to my police contact on the island and ask people to look out for someone dressed as a creepy shepherd in case that brings in any leads," he said. "I do not think the general public is in danger right now, and I'm not going to release the fact he was after Joey." Finally, his eyes met hers again. "Also, I'm not going to let you and Joey out of my sight again until this is over. Unless you're safely at home, with the doors locked, or in the company of somebody else we trust to keep you safe, you're with me. Got it?"

Something tightened in her chest. "Got it."

She could tell that Finnick wanted to carry Joey on the walk home. But she wasn't ready to let him go, so instead, he just helped her tighten the straps of her carrier and then, as they walked, stuck so close to her side that the hems of their jackets might as well have been stitched together. First they collected Casey's shopping bags from where she'd dropped them in the snow. Then they doubled back to the Candy Cane Bed and Breakfast, taking Main Street this time, although the sights and sounds of Christmas moved past Casey in a blur. The choir was still singing and now Drew had joined his wife and daughters in belting out carols. The family smiled and waved to them as they passed. Sweet smiles beamed on the three girls' rosy faces. Farther down the road, Patrick and his son, Tristan, were diligently tackling a block of ice together with hammers and chisels for an ice-carving competition. Casey's brother-in-law, David, stood in front of the community church, handing out candy canes and flyers reminding people of the Christmas Eve nativity play and Christmas morning service. Eileen was still in front of the bed-and-breakfast—now berating Cameron for wandering off at the wrong moment and missing the unveiling of a new gingerbread house. But she abruptly stopped when she saw Casey and Finnick approach.

Eileen ran over. Her hands fluttered as she asked Finnick if he was ready to resume the tour, if he'd decided to take a room at Candy Cane, and what Nippy had gone off running after.

"A rat." Finnick said, answering her last question and ignoring the other two. "And if you'll excuse me, I'm going to walk Casey home."

Casey expected her sister to argue, having never once known Eileen to back down. But it must've been the fact she still suspected Finnick was a judge, the authority in Finnick's voice, or a combination of both, that had her flapping her hands some more and telling Casey to bring him to all the events. She told them she'd see them later.

As Casey, Finnick, Joey and Nippy were walking out of town, a roar of cheers rose behind them, and it took her a second to realize why. The power had come back on. Christmas lights flickered to life on houses ahead of them. A snowplow approached them at a crawl, clearing the road as it passed and moving toward town.

The wind picked up too and blew through the freshly plowed road toward them, leaving powder in its wake. Nippy raised his snout and sniffed the wind. They kept walking, and a few minutes later, she heard something buzz in Finnick's pocket. He yanked out his phone and smiled.

"Good news," he said. "The phones are

back. Hopefully, that means we'll have the bridge to the mainland back too."

"Hopefully," she said and tried to smile. But the word felt hollow on her tongue.

When the bridge was open, Joey would leave, followed by Finnick and Nippy, and she'd be alone again. Which was fine. She was used to being alone, and they had their lives to live without her.

Still. The thought sat heavy in her heart.

Finnick placed a quick call to the police chief and filled him in on what had happened to Casey. After some back and forth, they decided not to alert the public that there was a man running around dressed like a shepherd.

"The costume isn't the threat," Finnick explained to Casey after he ended the call. "The man is. And if we get the whole island looking for that specific outfit, he'll just ditch it and switch to wearing something else. It's to our advantage that he keeps wearing that outfit as long as possible and doesn't switch disguises on us, assuming both attacks were done by the same man."

"It definitely seemed like the same guy," Casey said. "His voice was distorted, like he was using something to make it deeper than usual. But I definitely recognized it."

They kept walking through the snow, back toward her house, and they found themselves having to slow their steps every few moments to keep pace with Nippy. The dog was still sniffing the wind, and more deliberately, with his ears perked. It seemed there was some scent on the air he was able to detect now, which he hadn't smelled before. Finnick glanced at the K-9.

"Everything okay?" he asked the dog.

Nippy whimpered slightly and tossed his head in frustration.

"That means he's not sure what he smells," Finnick said. "Or the scent is too faint to detect. There might be a dead raccoon nearby."

Finnick turned back to his phone, and because Casey hadn't brought hers, she had nothing to check as he scrolled through messages.

"I missed a meeting with the team," he said. "I'm going to have to try to reschedule it, and of course we're going to have to call the social worker. But my team has started chasing some leads and are reporting in what they've found." He scrolled a few more moments, then stopped short and grabbed her hand. "I think we've found Ally."

"Really?" Casey asked. "That was fast."

She turned toward him, and for a moment, his finger lingered on hers as he held his phone up between them with his other hand. There on the screen was the smiling picture of a young, blonde woman, with a baby who looked an awful lot like Joey in her arms.

"Her name is Ally Wilson," Finnick said, and they kept walking. "She works as a waitress at a dive bar near a Sudbury casino. Seven weeks ago, she gave birth to a baby boy named Joey. No father on the birth certificate, but she told fellow waitresses it was a customer. She didn't make it home last night and didn't show up for her shift today."

Casey's mouth gaped.

"How could someone on your team find all that out so fast?" she demanded. "It took police months and months before they were even convinced that Tim and Stella's disappearance might've been foul play. You didn't even search my property with Nippy until he'd been gone almost a year. And now your team finds all this out overnight?"

Finnick's jaw tightened and for a moment it looked like he was trying to swallow something that tasted bad.

"My first hire for the Cold Case Task Force," he said, "is a private investigator named Gemma. She doesn't think like a cop and can get through the kind of doors that are reluctant to let police in. She figured that if Tim was still alive, he'd be frequenting some pretty lousy dumps full of the kind of people who don't call the cops, so she started calling around to a bunch of them, asking about Ally. She was at it all night and eventually she called the right dive at four in the morning and a worried friend of Ally's answered the phone."

Casey blinked.

"That's incredible," she said. "Where was she when Tim and Stella went missing?"

"High school," Finnick said. "My team are all in their twenties."

They'd reached Casey's farmhouse. She turned and started down the path Finnick had dug in the snow, back to her front door. Finnick began to follow.

Nippy barked loudly, and they turned around. The dog's nose was straining toward the road ahead of them. His paws were dancing on the snow. Then Nippy barked again, this time more urgently than before.

Finnick's face paled.

"What is it?" Casey asked.

"Nippy detects something," Finnick said. "Not a raccoon, a person. And whoever it is, they're dead."

A chill ran down Finnick's spine that had nothing to do with the cold, and for a moment he almost found himself hoping that the K-9's keen senses were wrong.

Nippy whimpered and pawed the ground impatiently.

"I hear you," Finnick told him. His gaze followed the direction the dog was indicating and saw what looked like a cabin in the distance. Its wood was gray and faded with age.

"What's that?" he asked Casey.

"That's the original one-room cabin that Tim's great-grandfather lived in while he was building the main house and barn," she said. "There have been Thompsons living on this property for over a hundred years. When Tim's father was a kid, apparently he and the other kids used to all camp out there in sleeping bags. But now the roof is mostly missing and the floor-boards are rotten. Tim always said we'd restore it when we had the money, for our own kids."

Her voice hitched and Nippy barked again. Seemed the K-9 was certain there was something in that cabin now that he wanted Finnick to see. And what they found there wasn't going to be good. He glanced down at Joey. The little boy had fallen asleep again with his head nestled peacefully against Casey's heart, and Finnick suspected the child could hear it beating.

"All right, I'm torn about what we do," Finnick said. "I want you to go in the house and lock the door. But I also don't want to leave you alone in there until I've had a few moments to search it and make sure there's nothing to worry about—"

"I'm going with you to see what's in the cabin," Casey cut him off firmly. "It's on my property and I can tell you if anything's off since the last time I was there."

"Okay," Finnick said and nodded. "But promise me you'll stay back."

"I will."

They left the path that Finnick had shoveled earlier and cut through the deep snow, single file, following Nippy's lead. After a few minutes they were able to see indents in the snow, letting them know that somebody had made their way to the cabin, by taking a different path from the road hours earlier, dragging something behind them. But so much snow had fallen since then, it was impossible to make out any distinct footprints or know exactly what they'd dragged. The door to the cabin lay open, sideways on broken hinges. Finnick called Nippy to heel and then stepped inside.

A woman lay on the floor, huddled up in a ball. Blond hair fell over her face. Her hands cradled a bloody gunshot wound to her stomach, which he was sure had been fatal. His heart lurched.

"Hello?" he called softly, even as he knew he wasn't going to get an answer. "I'm here to help you."

Finnick took a deep breath, walked toward her. Behind him, he could hear a soft gasp leave Casey's lips and her footsteps falter on the wooden floor, but he didn't let himself look back. He had a job to do—one of the hardest he ever had to do.

Nippy whimpered, his head bowed.

"Good job," Finnick said sadly and ran his hand down the K-9's side. "Good dog."

Then Finnick crouched down, gently reached out a gloved hand and touched the woman's arm. It was cold and stiff to the touch. He brushed the hair back from her face.

It was Ally.

The woman whose face he'd seen for a fleeting second the night before in his van headlights and then again in the picture Gemma had sent. She now lay dead on the cabin floor. A wallet bulged from her jacket pocket. He eased it loose to double-check he was right and found her employee identification card from work alongside her driver's license. He sighed. Just moments ago, he'd found a lead and now she was already gone.

Lord, please have mercy on all those who loved her, and help me bring the one who hurt her to justice.

He stood up slowly and turned to Casey again. Her arms were wrapped around Joey, holding him tightly to her. Finnick walked toward her and gestured for her to step outside.

"It's Joey's mother, Ally," he said. "She's been dead for hours."

"I don't understand," Casey said. "She was seen getting into a van driving out of Juniper Cove."

Casey's eyes were still locked on Ally's body. Finnick reached out his hand, took

Casey's arm gently and led her through the snow toward the house.

"I don't know what happened," Finnick said. "I'm guessing the person whose vehicle she got into killed her and dumped her here."

Finnick wondered if the killer was trying to frame Tim. Although, he wasn't sure how that fit with Ally thinking that Tim was the father of her child. He could feel Casey shaking under his touch and reminded himself of his promise to keep an open mind about everything.

"There's a lot we don't know right now," he said. He steered her back onto the path he'd dug. "So we've just got to focus on putting one foot ahead of the other, and on taking the next step. Right now, you're going to get Joey inside, change him, feed him, play with him and make sure he's all good. And I'm going to call the police and get them here to process the scene and take care of Ally. I'm also going to call the social worker from CPS and let them know that Joey's mother has passed away."

Casey nodded again and he watched as her chin rose in determination.

Everything looked exactly as they'd left it inside the farmhouse, down to the streaks of water the dishes had left on the counter. Still, Finnick did a complete sweep of the house, double-checking each room, window and door lock, before leaving Casey inside to take care of Joey.

He stepped out, called the chief of police and quickly filled him in. Finnick placed a call to Child Protective Services next and then fired off a message to his team letting them know about Ally. After, he and Nippy walked back to the cabin and stood in the doorway, keeping watch over Ally's fallen form. Finnick prayed until he finally saw two police cars and a third unmarked vehicle pull up.

Moments later, Chief of Police Rupert Wiig, stepped out of the unmarked car and headed across the snow toward him. The old man's hair and full beard seemed even whiter than the snow. He had the build of a man who had been a force to be reckoned with in his youth and had since spent many years eating an abundance of good food and sitting in a very comfortable armchair. If Finnick were to guess, he'd have pegged his age at least a decade, or even two, past when he could've retired. He was soon followed by two young men and a young woman in their twenties. Two police officers and a crime scene investigator, judging by their uniforms. They reminded Finnick of his own new team. There was a slight jog in Rupert's step, like he was determined to reach Finnick before the younger trio did.

"Hello, my old friend!" Rupert called, with only the slightest sign of exertion in his breath. "I'm so sorry about all this. I'm sure this isn't the kind of scene you expected to stumble into when you decided to visit the island to do some last-minute Christmas shopping."

So, did that mean that Rupert had opted not to tell the rest of the team that there was another senior cop visiting the island?

Either way, Finnick was going to go with it.

"No indeedy!" Finnick called back.

"We've got an ambulance on the way too," Rupert said, "but I won't call for it until we're ready to move the body. The island only has two ambulances, and the island's tiny hospital is completely over-loaded, with the people who've spun out on the ice driving or fallen while shovel-ing. They can't get any backup in because the bridge to the mainland is still closed and not expected to reopen until tomor-row now."

So that meant neither he nor Joey were going anywhere soon.

Nippy wagged his tail and woofed loudly at Rupert in greeting.

"Why, is that Nippy?" Rupert exclaimed. "You were just a tiny pup when I saw you last."

"Well, now he's getting old like the rest of us," Finnick said.

"Speak for yourself!" Rupert retorted. The two veteran police officers clasped each other's hands in a warm two-handed shake. Then Rupert stepped back as the three younger people arrived and stood smartly behind him, waiting for instruction.

"What can you tell us?" the cop who'd reached them first asked. He was about twenty-four with snow in his black curly hair. And since the officer hadn't offered up his name, Finnick didn't feel like he had to offer his.

"We were walking back from town when the dog started fussing that he smelled something," Finnick said. "I wondered if it was a raccoon. We wandered over here and found the body."

"Did you touch her or disrupt the scene in any way?" the female crime scene investigator asked.

Finnick noted both cops had now pulled

pads from their pockets and had begun taking notes.

"Just her wrist to confirm she was dead and her wallet to get her name," Finnick said. "Ally Wilson. I was wearing gloves the entire time."

"And what brought you to Juniper Cove?" the first cop followed up.

"Well, it's definitely not because I was roped in to judge Juniper Cove for the Whimsical Christmas competition," Finnick said, and faked what he hoped was a realistic-looking nervous-civilian grin. "So, anyone who tells you that has got their wires crossed."

Nods spread between the law enforcement officers, then the trio moved inside to process the scene. Finnick's forced smile faded as they walked into the cabin.

He raised an eyebrow at Rupert, who gestured him away from the cabin.

"Nice save," Rupert said. "If I didn't know any better I'd have believed you were a rattled civilian who'd just stumbled upon his first corpse."

"I didn't know we were keeping law enforcement in the dark," Finnick said.

"Don't misunderstand. They're all amazingly talented." Rupert crossed his arms. "But the biggest threat law enforcement faces on an island like this is gossip. And I've learned not to take any unnecessary risks after how badly we bungled the Stella Neilson and Tim Thompson disappearance."

"So, you blame the cops for the fact the case went cold?" Finnick asked.

"Wouldn't be much of a cop if I didn't blame myself for the cases that don't get solved," Rupert said. "I wish you and your task force all the best. But from my point of view, the biggest obstacle you're going to be up against is what 'everybody already knows' about the case." He released his arms just enough to make air quotes. "Because whenever 'everybody knows' something to be true, it usually turns out that nobody actually knows a fool thing about what they actually witnessed or saw for themselves. They're just repeating what they've heard. If forty-nine people see a barn cat went walking through town this afternoon, but one particularly gifted storyteller thinks they see a leopard, by tomorrow morning, my phone will be ringing off the hook with a hundred people who'll pledge on their lives they saw spots, claws and fangs." Rupert snorted. "Do I sound jaded?"

"No, this is helpful," Finnick said, "and a timely reminder that for the cases my team tackles, public opinion will probably be already baked in. So, what does everybody know about Tim and Stella's disappearance?"

"According to my wife, what 'everybody knows' and no one will tell you, is that Stella was never good enough for our golden boy, Drew," Rupert said. "Her parents were mainlanders who moved here, but Drew's a third-generation islander.

He's much better off with Jessica, and their three girls are precious. Also that Stella was trouble. She was heard fighting with Drew before she took off with another man. They're just surprised it was Tim she left with and not Patrick."

"Drew and Stella had a fight before she disappeared with Tim?" Finnick asked. "Why have I not heard that before?"

"Because you're a mainlander and a cop," Rupert said. "Nobody's going to admit to a cop that they're glad Stella left the island. That would look heartless or suspicious. Especially if it turns out that the reason she's gone is that something bad happened to her. But they'll gossip to an old cop's wife."

"And what does island gossip say about Tim?" Finnick pressed.

"Some say that Stella manipulated him," Rupert said. "Some say Tim took advantage of her. Most think she was cheating on Drew with him. And everybody loved Drew."

"And some think she was cheating with Patrick too?" Finnick asked.

"Some do," Rupert said. "The young man had a reputation."

"What kind of reputation?" Finnick pressed.

"Patrick and his former girlfriend had a baby outside of wedlock," Rupert said, "which people thought showed a lack of morals on his part." Finnick remembered what Casey's sister, Eileen, had said about Joey's mother. "Fair or not, a man doesn't shake a reputation like that in a place like this. Again, this is just island gossip. I'm not claiming for one moment there's any truth to any of it. Take it with a big grain of salt."

"Will do."

There was a flurry of exclamations coming from the cabin behind them. Seemed the investigation team had found something important.

"Hey, Chief," a cop called. "We've found something."

Rupert turned and walked into the cabin, with Finnick and Nippy a step behind him.

"She had this in her pocket," the crime scene investigator said. She held up a white, rectangular piece of plastic.

On the front was a picture of Tim Thompson with his name under the name of a hardware store.

It was Tim Thompson's employee key card.

SIX

Casey gently lowered a drowsy Joey into his crib, eased her hands away from his tiny body and then stood back, hoping he wouldn't wake up. It had been almost an hour since Finnick had left her alone in the house and headed back to the cabin. Since then, she'd fed Joey, changed him, and then gave him time to wriggle and kick on his play mat while she made herself a simple lunch of soup and bread, then wrapped the Christmas presents she'd bought in town and set them on the mantel. Soon, the small baby's eyes had begun to close again. No doubt he was tired out from all the fresh air and excitement of the morning.

Casey stepped back, waiting to see if

he'd settle into a deeper sleep. Instead, his blue eyes snapped open, his face scrunched into a grimace, and he began to wail.

"Shh shh shh shh shh…" Casey hushed the babe softly and laid one hand on his chest. "Everything's okay, Honey Bun. I'm here."

She stood there for a long moment, keeping her breath gentle and her voice soothing until finally Joey's cries quieted and his eyes began to close again. Casey exhaled slowly and pulled away. She dropped down onto the rug, curled up beside him and watched him sleep, not quite ready to leave him.

How much longer would this precious baby be in her life?

She'd called the social worker while Joey had been playing. Thankfully, Finnick had already called her to fill her in about Ally's death. At the time, she'd been too busy caring for the baby to really let herself dwell on what the social worker had been saying. But now, alone in the silence of the darkened bedroom, the social worker's words ran relentlessly through her mind.

To Casey's surprise, according to the social worker, their local broken swing bridge had made both national and international news, with dramatic pictures of the jackknifed transport van hanging half-off the bridge, with the beautiful frozen lake below and snowy island behind it. Although the ice near the shore on each side was thick enough for ice fishing and ice-skating, it wasn't strong enough for people to cross all the way from one side to the other. And a dramatic buildup of cars had formed on both sides of the bridge with people desperate to get on to be the first to cross when it reopened.

"It's expected to reopen in the middle of the night or early tomorrow," the social worker had said, "at the earliest. So, I'm just going to hold tight here until traffic is moving smoothly again. In the meantime,

I'm looking for a more permanent home for Joey. Now that we know his full name and that his mother is dead, we can see if there's a relative on either his mother's or his father's side who can take him, or we can plan to relocate him into a foster home near his remaining family."

Presuming CPS was able to identify the father. There were a lot of kids in the system, and even many who were put up for adoption, who's fathers were never known or identified. Often for tragic and criminal reasons.

"I know you'd probably happily keep the little tyke forever," she added and at this, the social worker's voice had softened, "but there's a lengthy process we need to go through, including first ruling out if both families are potential caregivers for him, and confirming they don't intend to be actively involved in his life."

Casey had told the social worker that she understood, and of course, she had. Social services always tried to place children with family. It was a slow process on purpose. When one of the parents was still alive, even if they were in prison for the worst of crimes, if that parent didn't voluntarily give up parental rights, it could take years for the courts to strip them and make a child available for adoption.

"The mother was from Sudbury and there are a lot of good foster families there," the social worker had reassured her, "as well as an excellent team of pediatricians we work with. Joey will be well cared for."

"You will be well cared for," Casey whispered to the sleeping child.

She clung to the promise of those words, closed her eyes and began to pray.

Lord, this precious child has been abandoned by a mother who he's now lost forever. Please, keep Joey safe. Empower Finnick and I to keep him safe for as long as he's in our care. Prepare the family You have planned to raise him as their own. May it be filled with wonderful peo-

*ple who love You, love each other, and
will love Joey and protect him as I would.*

*And please, when the time comes, give
me the strength and peace I need to let
them go.*

Casey hadn't meant to fall asleep there
on a rug, on the floor of her spare bedroom. She didn't even realize that she had
until she slowly opened her eyes again
to find that she felt more rested, renewed
and invigorated than she had when she'd
drifted off. The door she'd left open had
been closed. A pillow had been placed
under her head while she'd been sleeping
and a soft quilt tucked around her body,
enveloping her in its cocoon. Her watch
told her almost forty minutes had passed
since she brought Joey in to sleep.

Finnick must've checked on her and
found her there.

More than that, he'd taken care of her.

An odd and unfamiliar warmth filled
her body—not just from the quilt itself but

from the knowledge that someone cared enough to gently tuck it around her.

She stood slowly and crept to the door as quietly as she could so as not to wake the still sleeping child. She eased the door open silently and closed it behind her.

Faint voices trickled down the hallway from the living room.

"I don't know why you guys are all dancing around the fact that we have a clear and obvious suspect here." The voice was male, frustrated and unfamiliar. "The victim, Ally Wilson herself, wrote Casey Thompson a letter claiming that Tom Thompson was her child's father. We have evidence, motive and a clear pattern."

"How do you figure that, Caleb?" This new voice was female and equally frustrated.

Casey began to creep down the hallway toward the living room.

"Ally Wilson and Stella Neilson were both young women," the male voice argued. "Both have a connection to Tim Thompson—"

"Allegedly," the female voice cut in.

"—and both are either dead or vanished," he went on. "They were about the same age. Stella was last seen with Tim. Ally tried to blackmail Casey Thompson with the fact that she had a baby with Tim. Casey is attacked by a man claiming to be Joey's father."

Casey reached the end of the hallway. Nippy was stretched out on his side in front of the fireplace with his eyes closed. Finnick was sitting on the couch with his back to her and his laptop open on the trunk that served as a coffee table. Four video chat boxes were open on the screen showing three men and one woman.

"Clearly, there's a pattern here." The voice came from a blond man in the upper-right corner of the screen, who she assumed was Caleb. "For all we know, Stella was also pregnant with Tim's child and planning on blackmailing him or Casey."

"Now you're just pulling theories out of a hat!" The woman's voice rose. She had short brown hair and was waving both hands at the screen for emphasis. "Jackson, Lucas, Finnick. Somebody back me up here!"

A man with brown hair and a beard chuckled. "I know better than to cut in when you're on a roll, sis."

Finnick hit the volume button to turn them down, no doubt thinking she was still asleep. But Casey had already been eavesdropping longer than she should have. She cleared her throat and Nippy's head rose in her direction, but Finnick's eyes were still focused on the screen.

"Gemma, she had Tim's key card on her!"

"That means nothing!"

"Who had Tim's key card?" Casey asked.

Finnick leaped up quickly and shut the laptop, cutting off the conversation.

"Casey, hi!" Finnick looked flustered,

almost apologetic. "I was just talking to my team."

He turned back to the laptop as if noticing for the first time he'd accidentally shut it. His eyes closed for a long moment as if praying silently. Then when he opened them again, they were clear and unflinching. And somehow she knew that he wasn't going to beat around the bush in what he told her, which was both scary and comforting.

"Come sit." He patted the empty space on the couch beside him. "I'll show you what we found, get your thoughts on it and then I'll reconnect to the team call and introduce you to everyone."

He moved over on the couch as she sat down beside him.

Finnick opened a picture on his phone and then handed the device to Casey. She stared down at the laminated key card in the picture for a long moment. Every little detail brought back a flood of memories, from the slightly goofy smile that showed

Tim had been caught off guard when his picture was taken, to the way the last few letters of his last name were scrunched on the signature line when he ran out of space, to the way the top loop of the card was torn from how he'd kept ripping the lanyard clip off and duct-taping it back together.

"I also took a picture of the back if you'd like to see it," Finnick said, "but it's nothing but a scratched-up magnetic strip."

"No need," Casey said. "It's definitely his. He used to leave it behind all the time and then call me to come bring it to him." She handed the phone back to him. "Where was it?"

"In Ally's pocket."

Casey gasped in a painful breath that seemed to sting all the way down to her core.

No wonder someone on Finnick's team would assume that Ally was telling the truth about Tim being Joey's father.

Finnick's phone began to ring, alerting

him that his team was trying to reconnect him to the video call. Casey wondered if they'd been politely giving him time before calling back. Or if they'd been so locked in their debate about the potential significance of Tim's key card it had taken them this long to notice the call had dropped.

Finnick hesitated.

"Go ahead," she said. "No need to keep them waiting."

Finnick opened the laptop and accepted the call on his computer app. The four faces she'd seen earlier flickered back to life in separate boxes. Although now she could see that the young woman in the top left corner had the same brown hair and expressive blue eyes as the man in the box beneath her, who'd called her sis. On closer inspection, they seemed to be sitting on opposite ends of the same couch.

"Hi, guys, this is Casey," Finnick said. She waved in greeting and they waved back. "Going clockwise around the circle, top left is Gemma Locke, the best private detective I've ever met and the one who was up at four in the morning tracking down Ally's identity for us.

"The man in the square beside her is Officer Caleb Perry, who spent years as a beat cop before I met him as a rookie K-9 officer."

And whose brow was still knit in frustration over something.

"Below him is Lucas Harper." Finnick gestured to a man with a dark beard and even darker eyes, who Casey realized was the only one who hadn't spoken up during the banter earlier. "He used to work with the special victims unit and that yellow Lab rolling around behind him on the floor is his arson K-9, Michigan. Lucas actually contacted me and asked if he could join the team when he heard a rumor about the task force being founded.

"Which brings us back to Jackson Locke—" Finnick pointed to the last square "—brother of Gemma and one of the finest K-9 officers I've ever had the privilege of working with. He's not officially part of the team yet and is still getting up to speed."

They all exchanged a fresh round of hellos.

"I've asked Casey to look at a picture of the key card," Finnick went on, "and she identified it as Tim's. While we have her here, do any of you have any questions for her about it?"

"Is it possible Tim didn't have his key card with him on the day he disappeared?" Lucas asked. His voice was calm, and although he wasn't smiling, there was something reassuring about the steadiness of his tone. "Could he have left it at work?"

Casey shook her head. "He would've needed it to lock up that night."

Caleb leaned forward and rested his elbows on an unseen table.

"I'm sorry if you were offended if you overheard me say something about your husband being our obvious suspect—" he started.

"Late husband," Casey interjected.

"Former husband who has been legally declared dead," Caleb corrected himself, and his tone softened, "but, believe it or not, I'm not unsympathetic to what you've been through. I once dated a woman who I was warned about, and I refused to believe it. Then she murdered someone, and I've always blamed myself for not seeing it sooner." His gaze moved from Casey to Finnick. "I just want to make sure we're not being blind to the obvious truth of what's going on here, just because it's uncomfortable for some people to believe."

"I hear you," Finnick said, "and you're right that we all need to keep an open mind about this until it's solved. In the meantime, I want you to track down every possible shred of evidence you can find that Ally was involved in a relationship with Tim, and anyone else she might've been involved with. I'm still hopeful I'll see you all at Gemma's tomorrow night. But first I need to get off this island and get a new windshield installed in my van."

"If you were here, I'd be able to pop out the old windshield and install a new one for you myself," Lucas said. "I worked at my grandpa's garage all throughout high school."

"I thought he was fire chief," Caleb asked.

"That was my dad," Lucas said, with a grin.

A cheerful squeal sounded somewhere off-screen. Jackson reached down, scooped something up into his arms and sat back up with the baby on his lap. She was about six or seven months old, with short curls and a giant smile.

"This is Skye, my fiancée Amy's daughter," Jackson said. His smile grew as wide as the child's. "Amy and I have already started the adoption paperwork so we can finalize it as soon as we get married. Amy's working at the bookstore right now but wanted me to tell you she's looking forward to seeing you all at Christmas too."

Cheerful exchanges about upcoming Christmas plans went around the group, and the call ended shortly afterward in a fresh flurry of goodbyes. Finnick closed the laptop again. He leaned his elbows on his knees and clasped his hands together, as if silently praying. Once again, she had the sense Finnick was choosing the next words he was about to speak carefully.

"I'm not going to go into the depths of somebody else's business," Finnick said after a long moment, "because it's not my story to tell. But Amy's ex-husband, Skye's father, was a criminal and a pretty nasty piece of work. I know it's hard to look at a beautiful child, like Skye or Joey, and imagine there's a sad history behind how they came into the world. But I believe God can create beauty and hope out of every human tragedy. If I didn't,

I wouldn't have the strength I need to do this job."

"Does that mean you really are keeping an open mind about the fact Tim might've killed Stella and Ally?" she asked.

"I'm honestly doing my best to keep an open mind to everything," Finnick said, carefully, "including the fact Tim might still be alive."

"Well, I can't," Casey said.

She stared down at her own knees. They were barely an inch away from Finnick's. Their hands were so close it would take nothing for either of them to reach out and take the other's. And yet, it felt like there was a huge, impassable gap between them.

Lord, am I wrong to cling so tightly to what I believe is true? Having an open mind feels impossible right now. But help me be open and willing to see whatever You want to show me.

"I want you to know that regardless of what you overheard, I am confident my entire team is also keeping an open mind," Finnick added. "I have, and might, ask them to try to prove or disprove certain theories. But I have faith in them and I know they won't let bias impact their work."

The team seemed both very competent and very close. She wasn't completely sure what they thought of her though.

"Not even the square-chinned blond cop who looked like the obvious secret villain on a police procedural?" Casey asked bitterly and then immediately regretted saying something so unkind.

"Caleb?" Finnick chuckled suddenly, as if she'd managed to surprise him so thoroughly the laugh just exploded out of his lungs. "I hope when this is all over, you'll give me permission to tell him that. Because, again when this is all over, he'll probably get a kick out of someone saying he looks like a secret villain. Caleb can be a bit stubborn about his views on things, but he has a pretty good sense of humor about himself and has to put up with the others teasing him about being the team's 'handsome hero cop' cliché."

He seemed so confident that not only would everything they were going through be solved one day but that they'd all still be able to smile. It was almost comforting.

"Well, he's not my idea of handsome," Casey said, "but I'm definitely not going to hold that against him."

Finnick turned to face her and ran a hand over his jaw. "And what is your idea of handsome?"

You.

The single word crossed her mind so quickly it startled her.

But it was true. Sure, she'd been really attracted to Tim's youthful energy and eager grin. But there was something so specifically handsome about Ethan Finnick that went deeper than the strong lines of his jaw, the echo of his earlier laughter, which glinted like gold in his dark eyes, and the way his fingers traced the curve of his smile. Finnick was attractive in a way that tugged at something inside her chest that she hadn't felt in years, like the chain of an old dusty lamp being pulled with just the right touch to bring the light back to life.

Finnick's smile faded slightly, but the warmth in his eyes seemed to deepen.

Heat rose to her cheeks as she desperately tried to think of a flippant answer to his question or even find a way out of the conversation.

Could he read her mind? Did he know she felt this way?

Then Finnick shot to his feet as if he'd suddenly realized he'd sat on a beehive.

"I noticed you wrapped some Christmas presents," he said, walking around the trunk and looking at the fireplace, leaving her to stare at his back. "Did you do that while I was talking to the police at the cabin?"

"Yeah, I did." Casey stood too and walked the opposite way around the trunk.

"I bought a few little things for Joey from the Christmas market. I know he'll probably be long gone by Christmas Day, and that he's too young to even remember his first one, but I still want him to know that he's loved. Even if I don't have a tree to put them under."

"Do you want to go cut one down?" Finnick turned back.

The suggestion was so sudden she laughed.

"You mean right now?" Casey asked.

"Why not?" Finnick asked.

"Because Joey's asleep and the Douglas fir grove we get our Christmas trees from is clear on the other side of the property."

"But there are pine trees not fifteen feet from the back door," Finnick said. "We can go chop one of those down and still be close enough to Joey that we'll be able to listen out for him. I can even park Nippy right in between the back door and bedroom door and ask him to alert if Joey stirs."

Casey bit her lip. The thought was more tempting than he knew. Thompson family tradition was they cut down a tree from the exact same spot every year. Due to the amount of work involved in trekking out there, cutting one down and dragging it back, she hadn't actually had a tree since Tim's disappearance. But cutting down one of the hundreds of others on the property felt like betraying relatives of Tim's who'd died before she was born.

Yet at the same time, it would be nice to have a tree. Especially for Joey's first Christmas.

"Okay," she said. "As long as we give up if Joey starts calling."

"Absolutely," Finnick said and grinned. "I'm going to go get something from my van. I'll meet you out back."

Not ten minutes later, Casey was standing on her back porch, in her winter boots, coat, hat and mitts, having confirmed not only that Joey was asleep but that the eight-foot pine tree she'd had her eyes on for years was less than twelve paces from Joey's window.

She heard Finnick behind her in the hallway, directing Nippy to lie down across Joey's bedroom door and keep watch, then he appeared in the doorway behind her.

"Ready to do this?" he asked.

She looked down in disbelief at the object in his hand. It was an old-fashioned metal axe with a wooden handle, so small it was probably more accurate to call it a hatchet. He twirled it like a lumberjack.

"I have a chainsaw in the garage," she said.

"Yeah, but it's not the same," Finnick said. "Have you picked out a tree?"

"That one." She pointed. "Unless you think it's too big."

"I think it's perfect."

They walked out into the snow and approached the tree. He handed the axe to her, handle first, and she took it. It was heavier than she expected.

"Have you never chopped down a tree?" he asked.

She thought for a moment.

"No. Come to think of it though," she said, "I've done a lot of carpentry and built my own worktable."

"Okay," he said. "Well, square off to where you want to hit the tree, grip it with both hands, take a step backward and then swing from your hips. Trust me, this will help."

Help what? she wondered.

But she stepped back as instructed and swung. The blade sliced cleanly into the tree trunk and stuck there with a satisfying *thwack*. She yanked it back hard, almost slipped but managed to maintain her balance and then steadied herself to swing again.

"I wouldn't admit this to most people," Finnick said. "I don't even think anyone on my team knows this about me. But when I'm overwhelmed and frustrated with everything at work, I go to my local gym and punch the heavy bag."

Another swing. Another *thwack*.

"I know a lot of people jog, walk or swim to clear their minds," Finnick went on, "and honestly, sometimes I feel like the oldest and slowest guy hitting a punching bag in a room full of twenty-year-olds. But something about the physical exertion helps. Even better when I can see myself accomplishing something."

"I get it." She swung again, watching as the axe cut deeper and deeper through the trunk. It was almost like the combination of rhythmic motion and physical effort was helping release the frustrations inside her. "I feel so trapped by all this sometimes." She swung again. "Like my life has been put on hold by something out of my control, and I'm forever going to be seen as the woman whose husband both vanished and might be a criminal."

The axe wedged so deep into the tree, it'd almost made it all the way through.

"For whatever it's worth, I don't see you that way," Finnick said. "I think..." He took a deep breath. "I think you're amazing, Casey."

She tried to yank the axe back, but it stayed firmly stuck within the trunk.

"You are unbelievably strong," Finnick continued, "and you've been through so much, and yet you still have such a kind and generous heart. You're just a beautiful—"

Casey braced one foot against the trunk and yanked again. The tree toppled over backward in front of her. The axe slipped from her hands. Casey lost her footing and tumbled backward, into Finnick's chest. His strong arms wrapped around her and held her close. His heartbeat thumped against her back. She turned her head to thank him, only to find his lips barely a breath away from hers.

"You're just a beautiful person, Casey," Finnick finished, and his voice grew husky in his throat. She could feel the heat of his breath on her face. "At least, that's who I see."

* * *

The sweet smell of Casey's hair filled Finnick's lungs as he held her tightly against his chest.

"Thank you," she whispered, and he felt her lips brush up against his cheek. "You're a pretty special person too."

She turned toward him. But he didn't step back and his arms didn't let her go. Instead, he just stood here, holding her to him. He could see her hazel eyes looking up into his and feel how the small of her back fit perfectly against his hands.

Casey leaned toward him. He leaned toward her too. And Finnick knew in that moment that, just as his van had careened off the road the night before, he was about to send his own heart and common sense into an equally unadvised tailspin.

He was about to kiss Casey Thompson. He was going to envelop her in his arms and let their lips finally meet in that kiss he'd first imagined when he'd grabbed her hand back in her kitchen over a decade before.

But before their lips could meet, Casey tucked her head into the crook of his neck and hugged him back tightly. "I'm so glad you're here and that I have you as a friend."

He swallowed hard, firmly shoving the reckless thought of kissing her away into the furthest recesses of his mind.

"Yeah," he said. "Me too."

And then all at once, Nippy began to bark, Joey began to cry and Casey pulled away and ran toward the house. Moments later when he stepped inside, he heard the sweet sound of Casey soothing Joey's tears and the baby calming in her arms.

He had almost kissed Casey.

Right. Now, that had almost been the most foolish thing he'd ever done.

Even though she'd never given him any indication that she wanted him to kiss her or that she would've kissed him back. Let alone the fact he'd never been the kind the guy who went doing things like that, even when he'd been in his twenties, no matter how attracted he was to someone.

And Casey was beyond attractive.

Lord, what's going on inside me? I've never been the kind of guy who let his heart get all tangled up in a woman. My team is looking to me for leadership. Help me get this case wrapped up and back to my team.

Whatever was going on inside him was beyond ridiculous. Casey's life was here on this island. His was with his team, running his task force, which was going to be based on the outskirts of Toronto. That was over six hours' drive away in good weather. Casey wasn't asking him to stick around on the island for her. And even if she ever did, there was no way he could stay.

I have prayed so long to open a cold case unit and I'm so confident that this new task force was Your answer to my prayer. Please, help me stay focused on the work You've called me to do.

Finnick turned and went back out to the tree, picked up the axe and gave it one final swing to sever the trunk from its stump. Then he dragged it through the snow to the back porch, where he set it up under the awning to dry off a bit before he'd bring it inside. Nippy was waiting for him, just inside the door, with his tail wagging.

Casey was in the bathroom. He watched, as he passed, as Casey ran a bath for Joey, singing to the baby as the water filled the small tub. Finnick went into the kitchen and ate the remnants of the soup and bread that Casey had left on the counter for him. He tidied the dishes, wiped the counter down, then sat at the kitchen table with his laptop and went back to working the case.

Gemma was still chasing down Ally's friends to see what more she could find out about Joey's father and the past few months of Ally's life. It seemed the young woman wasn't one for steady, long-term relationships, but she'd started dating what her friends called an "older man" recently, when the "cute younger guy" she'd been with had ended their relationship. Not much to go on, but Ally was still digging. Caleb and Lucas meanwhile had divided up the area around the bar where Ally worked and were checking local businesses for any sign of Tim Thompson. And while Jackson wasn't yet an official member of the task force, Finnick had gotten an email from the inspector who'd taken over from Finnick as head of the RCMP's Ontario K-9 Unit, letting him know Jackson had officially requested a transfer to join Finnick's team.

Disappointingly, Rupert and the local police hadn't been able to pull any usable fingerprints or DNA from Ally's body or where it was found. And while the team had been canvassing the area between Casey's cabin and where Ally was seen getting into a vehicle, they were still no closer to figuring out who had picked her up and how she'd gotten onto Casey's property.

Finnick looked over at his old, faithful partner. Nippy had repositioned himself next to Joey's play mat, with his snout on his paws, likely waiting for his new little friend to arrive after his bath. As if sensing Finnick's gaze on him, Nippy raised his head and fixed his dark eyes on Finnick, waiting for direction.

Rupert and his team might not be able to trace whoever had killed Ally and deposited her in the shed on Casey's property.

But Nippy could.

The smell of death could linger on fabric for a good twenty-four hours, including car interiors. If he took Nippy for a slow walk though Juniper Cove, maybe he could get the dog to track the vehicle the killer had used.

Finnick heard the sound of Casey's footsteps coming down the hallway. She was humming softly under her breath and from the patter of her steps on the wooden floorboards it sounded as if she was dancing. And he could feel something in his heart almost skip in time to the melody. He'd been back in her life less than a full day, and already, he'd become way too invested in whatever she was thinking or feeling.

Truth was his first impulse was always to tell her about whatever new lead or idea he had about the case. But she wasn't on his team and she wasn't law enforcement. And despite how incredibly comfortable he felt around her, she wasn't the person he rushed home to at night to tell about his day.

And he couldn't afford to let himself get distracted with thoughts about her now. That would have to wait. And he'd summon the self-control to make it wait. Because, for now, he needed to untangle her from this case. And from constantly being front and center in his thinking about it.

A moment later, Casey appeared, with

a freshly bathed Joey in her arms. He was dressed in a bright red onesie with smiling snowmen on it.

"I bought this for him at the Christmas market," Casey said. As she met Finnick's eyes, her smile was almost shy. A delicate pink glow rose to her cheeks. Had she realized just how close he'd come to kissing her? Then she broke his gaze and crouched down on the floor in front of the play mat, beside Nippy. "Thanks again for your help chopping the tree down. I think it was the reboot my brain needed. Everything's just been so dark and heavy for a long time. It'll be nice to bring a bit of Christmas joy back inside the house. Besides, you were right, there was something kind of therapeutic about it."

She laughed softly, but her eyes and smile were still fixed on the small child lying on the play mat in front of her.

"You don't mind if I leave you to take Nippy for a walk, do you?" Finnick asked. "I'm going to go later tonight when you and Joey are asleep. I mean, I've been walking him during the day, but I just wanted to double-check before I took him out at night."

"Oh, absolutely," Casey said. She was still looking at Joey. "I keep the doors locked now, and you definitely don't need to babysit me. After all, it's not like you'll be here keeping an eye on me forever." She laughed again, but something almost sad lingered at the edges of her voice. "Not that Joey has any concept on the difference between night and day yet. He was up screaming like a warrior at three in the morning. If I'd been able to get my van out of the garage last night, I'd have taken him for a drive up and down the road to settle him."

Okay then, that was settled.

The rest of the day passed in an easy and gentle kind of calm. Finnick helped Casey move the armchair away from the window and set the tree up in its place. Casey took care of Joey and searched the house and garage to dig out dusty boxes of Christmas decorations that clearly hadn't been opened in over a decade. And in between answering emails and phone calls, Finnick gave her a hand.

He spent most of the day on his laptop, coordinating with the team about how their investigations were going and confirming the final details about the building on the outskirts of Toronto, which the team would be moving into in early January when the task force formally launched. It was close enough to the highway to be able to pop downtown for meetings with other law enforcement entities or easily hit the road to Ontario's wild forests, dazzling lakes and hundreds of small towns. The two-story building had been a house once before being converted into offices. The old paint and carpets had left it feeling a bit shabby and rundown, but the bones were good.

There was a special kind of joy he felt, deep inside, seeing the final plans for the task force come together. He'd never been the type to have strong feelings one way or the other about paperwork. But as he scanned over the final sales agreement for the new headquarters, what the official parameters and scope of the task force would be and the official contracts for those joining his team, Finnick felt an incredible happiness filling his core.

This was what he'd prayed for and hoped for, ever since he'd been a rookie cop and working his first case. Now, in his late forties, just a few years away from when he could've taken early retirement, the door had finally opened for him to lead this team.

Lord, all my life You've been leading and guiding me to this moment. I can see Your hand in every step and I've never doubted the path You've laid out for me.

But then how did the gentle way his heart kept tugging him toward the woman and child now playing on the floor beside him fit into all that?

Dinner was a simple and cheerful meal of leftover bread from lunch and the meat pie that Casey had bought in town. The tree was half-decorated and Christmas garlands lay strewn across the couch and chairs, when Casey went to put Joey to bed just after eight.

"Feel free to keep decorating without me," she said with a tired smile before heading to the spare room. "It would be nice to have everything up for when the social worker comes tomorrow. I'll come join you when Joey falls asleep."

But Casey didn't come back into the living room. So, after half an hour, Finnick went to check on her and found her asleep on the floor beside the sleeping baby's crib again. Her hands were curled up underneath her head like a pillow. Her hair fell softly over the beautiful lines of her face.

His heart ached. That was twice now she'd fallen asleep on the floor watching Joey, her eyes almost level with his, as if she was afraid to let him out of her sight.

He crouched down beside her.

"Hey," Finnick whispered, feeling the simple word somehow catch in his throat.

"Ethan Finnick."

His name slipped her lips like a sigh, but her eyes didn't open. The knot in his throat grew.

"You fell asleep on the floor again," he said, softly. "You should really get a mattress for the floor if you're going to keep lying beside him. Do you want me to help you up?"

"Mmm-hmm, please."

Still her eyes didn't open. Was she even awake? Or was she talking in her sleep? He couldn't tell. He reached out to help her to her feet, but instead, she slipped her arms around his neck, suddenly dropping her weight into his arms. For a moment, his legs felt unstable beneath him. Then he lifted her up against his chest. Her head fell against his shoulder, her hair brushed his jaw and, once again, the scent of her filled his senses. And his lungs seemed to tighten in his chest. Finnick carried her down the hall into the living room, laid her down on the couch, draped a blanket over her and slid a pillow under her head. He double-checked that all the doors and windows were locked, called Nippy to his side and slipped back to his cot in the barn loft.

Finnick's plan was to set an alarm, sleep for a bit and then take Nippy out for a walk when Juniper Cove had fallen asleep. But despite the fact his faithful K-9 companion was quick to stretch out and start snoring, Finnick found himself lying awake on the cot for hours, staring at the wooden ceiling beams, unable to get the image of Casey curled up asleep on the floor, her face just feet away from Joey's.

There was something so strong and tough, and yet so fragile and tender, in the way Casey looked at the little boy. It was altogether beautiful.

He sighed. Were all the cold cases his task force investigated going to be this heart-wrenching? Or was there just something about this one case—this one woman—that got to him?

Lord, my heart aches for her, but I know that the wound inside her is something only You can heal. She got married and moved to this farm, planning on spending the rest of her life here raising a family. I have to have faith that You have a plan for her life, even in the face of disaster. Please, Lord, bring her peace. Bring her joy.

The world outside his window was empty and quiet by eleven, but still Finnick waited until almost one in the morning before carrying Nippy back down the stairs, putting his leash on and setting out into the night.

"Nippy." Finnick's voice was quiet and firm. "Search!"

The dog woofed softly in agreement and began to sniff the air. A bright white moon shone high above the winter's night, casting the snow around them in dazzling shades of silver and blue. They started walking down the street, the crunch of their footsteps seeming to echo in the silence of the night around them. Christmas lights flickered on and off from houses they passed, casting the shadows in red, green and gold. Slowly, they made their way down the street and through the residential neighborhoods of Juniper Cove. They passed the family homes Casey had pointed out earlier today, like the home of Drew and Jessica and their three daughters. A few doors down, they went by the much smaller bungalow where Patrick lived with his son, Tristan. As they reached Eileen and David's house, they saw a light was on in the apartment above the detached garage. Finnick and Nippy paused at the end of the driveway, and Finnick watched as Cameron's silhouette moved past the window. Apparently, Finnick wasn't the only one who couldn't sleep.

But no matter how keenly Nippy sniffed

the ground and smelled the air, the K-9 didn't detect the scent of death hanging on any of the homes or vehicles. Which Finnick knew he should thank God for, despite the fact that they were no closer to finding how Ally had gotten to Casey's shed. Eventually, they'd reached the end of Juniper Cove's homes and apartments, and finally looped around and began to walk through the shops and businesses on their way back to Casey's place.

The town had left its lights and displays on overnight, so that every corner still sparkled with holiday cheer, with no actual people there to celebrate it. All the trappings of Christmas, with no sign of life. The emptiness was eerie and reminded Finnick of when he'd wandered into an old-fashioned town inside the Chicago science center as a kid and wondered why all the people had vanished. And he found himself praying again.

Lord, for years I celebrated Christmas by working a double shift to make sure as many colleagues as possible could be home with their families. And every year it felt like the greatest gift I could give and my way of celebrating You. Lord, I don't know if it's Your will for Juniper Cove to win this competition or not. I just pray they won't lose sight of loving each other and You.

"Woof!" Nippy barked sharply, his voice suddenly piercing the stillness. Finnick looked down at his partner. The hackles rose at the back of Nippy's neck. His paws danced urgently on the ground and the dog barked again.

Nippy had found something.

"Show me," Finnick said.

Nippy woofed loudly and started running down the middle of snow-covered Main Street, kicking up fresh powder under his paws. Finnick ran one step behind. Nippy led him down a narrow lane between two buildings. It was slushy with old tire tracks and barely wide enough for a vehicle to pass one direction without clipping its mirrors. A metal chain-link fence, about eight feet tall, with a pad-locked gate lay ahead of them. Nippy ran straight for it. Motion sensor lights flickered on overhead. A plain white no-entry sign hung on the fence, telling Finnick it was the private property of Craft and Son Construction and that the main entrance was around the front of the building. The sole security camera was too covered from the recent downpour of snow and ice to catch anything, and it looked like it had been unplugged long ago.

Nippy leaped up at the fence, pawed the chain link and barked.

"I got it," Finnick said. "What you want me to see is on the other side of the fence. Good job."

He ran his hand over the back of Nippy's head and told him to sit. On the other side of the fence sat an empty lot that backed onto the construction building, with a few snow-covered piles of lumber off to the side and a single van about halfway across the parking lot. Judging by the lack of snow on top, it had been parked there recently. Then Finnick scanned the fence itself. The hinges weren't that strong. Probably wouldn't take much to break it open, but Finnick was only here for reconnaissance. That's how it went with undercover work. He'd find the evidence, call Rupert and let the island police move in with the warrant. He glanced behind him and scanned the alley. There was nowhere in the narrow alley that he could instruct Nippy to take cover, so he just instructed him to keep sitting.

Then Finnick leaped up, climbed the fence in four quick steps and dropped down the other side, feeling every muscle in his legs ache from the exertion. He stretched and felt his back crack.

"We never should've gotten old, bud," he told Nippy softly, who woofed softly in response.

Slowly, Finnick started across the snow and slush toward the van, careful not to

disrupt any of the tire tracks and footprints, not that he expected they'd be able
to pull anything usable from them. He
reached the van and shone his flashlight
inside. There were red stains on the floor
in the back.

Finnick blew out a breath. He couldn't
tell if it was blood, but it was definitely
enough to call Rupert and get a crime
scene investigator out here. He turned
and strode back across the empty lot toward the fence and Nippy. The dog's tail
wagged in greeting. Finnick reached for
his phone, then stopped. He'd hop the
fence, get reunited with his K-9 partner
and then make the call on their walk back
to Casey's. He'd already felt like he'd been
away from her and Joey too long.

The fence loomed ahead of him. Finnick
leaped up, climbed to the top and swung
his leg over the other side. Suddenly a van
honked behind him and headlights shot
to life, filling the path ahead of him with
light. Finnick looked back. They were no

longer alone. Someone had activated the van's remote starter.

A figure in robes and a rubber mask stood like a long, tall shadow in the beam. *The Creepy Shepherd.*

"Nippy!" Finnick shouted. "Run!"

The dog raced down the narrow alley, even as Finnick felt the instinct to jump down and charge at the man surge through his body. But before he even moved the figure raised a handgun and aimed it between Finnick's eyes.

He had a silencer on the weapon and the closest house was over a mile away. Finnick was alone. No backup. No team. The Creepy Shepherd could shoot Finnick dead right here and no one would ever know.

Lord, please save my life.

"Stop right there!" the Creepy Shepherd shouted. "I don't know who you think you are, poking your nose into my business, but you don't belong here. You leave this island and my family alone!"

Did he mean his literal business of Craft and Son? Did he mean Tristan?

Or was this somebody else? And if so, who was his family?

Casey? Joey?

Both?

"I can't do that," Finnick called back. "People have been hurt and all I'm trying to do is protect them. Why don't you put the gun down and we can talk—"

But before the word had barely left Finnick's mouth, the Creepy Shepherd set him in his sights and fired.

SEVEN

Finnick threw himself over the edge of the fence and plummeted down onto the ground below as the gunshot sounded through the air mere inches away from his head. Finnick's body smacked hard against the slushy ground. A second gunshot fired behind him, clanging off the metal chain-link fence and ricocheting into the darkness. The Creepy Shepherd swore and shouted threats. Between the cold, the darkness and the chain-link fence, it would be hard to get a direct shot. But his last two had been dangerously close. A third one might be fatal.

All Finnick could do was run.

He sprang to his feet and pelted down the alley, back toward Main Street, just in time to see Nippy disappear around the corner to safety. But just as he was breathing a prayer of thanksgiving that his partner was safe, he heard a van door slam and then an engine roar toward him. Finnick glanced back. The Creepy Shepherd had given up on the gun for now and had gone for the larger and blunter weapon—one he could be certain wouldn't miss.

He was going to run Finnick over.

Help me, Lord, I need You now!

Finnick pressed his legs to go faster. Behind him he heard the squeal of metal and a crashing noise as the van drove into the fence. Then came the sound of the vehicle backing up and driving forward again for a second blow. This time, he heard the gate fly off its hinges. The end of the alley loomed ahead. Only a few steps more and he'd be back on Main Street, but he was still blocks away from shelter, and whichever direction he ran the van would still be able to catch him. He heard the van drive over the fallen gate. The Creepy Shepherd was coming toward him.

Finnick burst out onto Main Street.

"Nippy!" he shouted.

The dog was nowhere to be seen and he could only pray Nippy found shelter.

Then a second pair of headlights pierced the darkness, racing down the road to his left and blinding him. He heard the screech of tires breaking on the snow and the most beautiful voice he'd ever heard calling his name.

"Finnick!" Casey shouted. "I've got Nippy! Jump in!"

He ran toward the sound of her voice, his eyesight cleared, and he spotted the passenger door of her van hanging open before him. Then he saw Casey with her hands on the wheel and her strong, determined eyes fixed on him. He dove in, scrambled into the seat and slammed the door behind him.

"Go!" he shouted. "Drive!"

Nippy woofed from behind him. Casey

hit the gas. Her van peeled down the empty street. Finnick struggled to clip his seat belt on and then glanced back. Nippy lay on the back seat with his head resting on the edge of the car seat where Joey lay fast asleep. Through the back window, he could see the van shoot out of the alley and race toward them.

"You followed me and put Joey and yourself in danger?" Finnick's voice rose.

"No, I didn't!" Casey's eyes cut to the rearview mirror. "But I'm not going to argue with you now. Who's chasing us?"

"The Creepy Shepherd." Fine, they could hash this out later. "He has a gun."

She fixed her eyes through the windshield ahead. The van sped down Main Street.

"And he's driving Patrick's delivery van?"

"Yeah." Finnick glanced back. The vehicle was gaining on them.

"Good," Casey said. He turned to look at her, and to his surprise, he caught the glimmer of a smile move through her voice. "Then, based on what Patrick told you this morning, the Creepy Shepherd's driving without decent snow tires."

Her hands tightened their grip on the steering wheel. They'd reached the edge of town now. Ahead of them lay the park with its dazzling tableau of sparkling lights, stretching from tree to tree in an endless maze of holiday splendor.

Casey steered straight for it. "Hang on," she said.

The ground grew steeper. The van grew closer until the glare of its headlights filled the van. Casey urged the van faster, pushing the accelerator down as far as she could. The other driver matched her speed. The lights of the park grew closer until they were only a few feet from the entrance. The van smacked against the back bumper, jolting them forward.

Casey yanked the steering wheel hard. The van spun on the icy street, and for a moment Finnick was afraid they were going to lose traction and fly off the road just as his van had done the night before. But instead, just as the tires began to slip, Casey righted the vehicle again and raced down the road parallel to the park. Finnick looked back, just in time to see the van careen straight off the road behind them, through the trees, and smash into a light display of dancing penguins.

Casey glanced at the rearview mirror. A long sigh of relief left her lungs and tears leaped to the corner of her eyes. Finnick's heart lurched, and he wanted to reach out to wipe them away before they reached her cheeks, but she swept her hand across her face before he could.

"It'll be easier for him to try to drive through the park than turn around," she said. "I'm not going to risk my life and Joey's chasing him. But I can drop you off at the far side."

"No," Finnick said, surprised to find that lump he'd felt hours before was back in his throat. "Please take me back to your house. I'm going to call Rupert and get the police to handle it. I'm not going to leave you alone again tonight. Nippy and I will sleep in the living room, and I'll ask Rupert to station someone on the road outside the house."

"Okay." She swallowed hard. "Thank you."

Her voice had dropped to a whisper, as if she had used up all her energy outrunning the van and now she was depleted. She glanced at the mirror again. The road lay dark and empty now. The van was gone.

He called Rupert, waking the police chief up, and filled him in on everything that had happened that evening. Rupert confirmed he'd have an officer on the street outside Casey's house the rest of the night. By the time he'd hung up the phone, Casey was pulling back into the farmhouse driveway. She cut the engine, and he realized she was shaking. He reached out his hand and rested it in between their seats, just inches away from hers, but she didn't take it.

"I meant what I said about not following you and not intentionally bringing Joey into danger," Casey said. "He woke up crying and wouldn't settle, so I took him for a drive in the van, down to Main Street and back. But when I reached Main Street, I saw Nippy tearing out of an alley way and heard what sounded like the pop of a gun that had the silencer on. So I got Nippy in the van and then found you." She shrugged and a small smile crossed her lips. "It's that simple."

Simple.

The word ran circles around in his brain later that night, as he lay on the couch in the living room, with Casey and Joey tucked in their beds down the hall. Nippy stretched out in front of the fire snoring, and the silhouette of an unmarked police car remained parked outside on the street.

He'd been in trouble, called out to God for help and Casey just happened to be nearby when he needed her. It sounded so simple. After all, she'd told him that if Joey didn't settle in tonight, she was tempted to take him for a drive, and Juniper Cove was pretty small.

But somehow, deep in his heart, it didn't feel simple at all. It felt downright complicated and confounding. This was hardly the first time somebody had been there in the right place at the right time. After all, he hadn't thought twice about the fact that he'd happened to crash onto Casey's farm the same night she was attacked by the Creepy Shepherd. He just saw that as God guiding his steps, just as God had done so many times before. Finnick had saved the lives of dozens and dozens of people in his life, and in return dozens of officers had saved his. It came with the territory.

And yet...

Lord, thank You for sending Casey to me when I needed her. Even though nothing I feel about her is simple. Despite the fact I've always believed in Your divine guidance, I don't understand why she tumbled into my life, and why I crashed into hers, right here and now. I don't have time to be in a relationship with anyone, and even if I did, her heart is tied to this island, hours away from where I'm founding my team.

But again, I thank You for bringing her into my life, in Your timing.

Whatever Your plan is for me.

Sleeping on the couch turned out to be more comfortable than he expected, despite the wheezy snores of the dog after their action-packed night. The sun was just beginning to rise when Finnick awoke. He checked his messages first and discovered that the bridge was still closed for a few more hours and that, although police had found Patrick's van had crashed through the ice and sunk into the lake, the man who'd been driving it dressed as the Creepy Shepherd was nowhere to be found.

Finnick prayed that, today, they'd finally get some answers. He got up, fed Nippy, checked his messages and started the coffee. Then he set about hanging up some of the garlands and Christmas decorations from Casey's boxes, focusing on the doorway arches, windows and high places she wouldn't be able to reach on her own without standing on something. After a while, he heard Joey's gentle cry coming from down the hall and the familiar sound of Casey scooping him up into her arms and singing to him as she got him dressed and ready to face the world. And somehow, Finnick knew that when tomorrow dawned, he'd miss them.

Moments later, Casey came down the hallway with Joey in her arms.

"Good morning!" she called, cheerfully. The rising sun seemed to dance in her eyes. Joey squealed and waved his arms in hello.

"Good morning." Finnick felt a slow grin cross his face.

"I'm guessing by the fact that you're not dancing around the tree that police didn't manage to catch the Creepy Shepherd last night?" she asked.

Finnick sighed sadly.

"No," he confirmed with a frown. "The van crashed into the lake and he managed to get out before it sunk. I'm guessing to destroy any of the evidence."

"And they probably won't have the equipment to get it out of the lake until the bridge reopens," Casey said as her smile dimmed. But a moment later, it returned as her gaze darted around the room and settled on a thick green garland with white dangling berries that he'd hung over the doorway between the living room and the kitchen. The corner of her mouth quirked. "I see you've been decorating."

He ran his hand over the back of his neck. Had he done something wrong?

"Yeah, I hope it's okay."

Her gaze finally landed back on his face. "It's great," she said. "Thank you."

"Well, I knew you wanted it done by the time the social worker gets here," he said. "Although, last I heard, the bridge still isn't open yet. They're expecting it to reopen later today."

And he'd finally be getting off the island and back to meeting up with his team. He was down to less than two weeks now until when the Cold Case Task Force would officially be launched and introduced to the country. There was still a huge amount of legwork to be done before that happened and there was only so much of it he could do while he was spinning his wheels in Juniper Cove. It would be up to the local police to process the van, although Finnick doubted they'd be able to pull anything from it after it had crashed into the lake.

The red stains he'd seen in the back would be long gone, with no way to know if they were even blood.

Casey slipped Joey into Finnick's arms and moved to the stove to start breakfast.

Finnick tucked the small child into the crook of his elbow and Joey brushed his tiny fingers across Finnick's jaw. Finnick swallowed hard.

"I'm going to miss you too, buddy," he whispered.

He sat down at the table, with one hand cradling the child and the other scrolling through messages from his team, as Casey whipped up a skillet of scrambled eggs and popped slices of fresh bread into the toaster.

"Can I give you a hand with any of that?" Finnick asked. "I may not be much of a cook, but I can whip a mean egg."

"No, I'm good," Casey said, and he could hear gratitude in her voice. "But if you could feed Joey, that would be great."

"No problem."

She wheeled around, and in what seemed like one seamless move, she grabbed the bottle from the warmer, doubled-checked the temperature on her wrist, dropped it into Finnick's waiting hand and then turned back to the eggs on the stove.

"Thankfully, I got the last of my Christmas orders off last week," Casey said, "and won't be starting on my spring soaps and candles until January. So, I've got plenty of free time right now to play with this little guy."

Joey took the bottle eagerly, and after trying a few different methods and angles, Finnick finally figured out how to feed Joey with one hand and check email with the other. A deep and sad sigh seemed to move through his core as he read the officers' reports. Lucas, Caleb and Gemma had turned up plenty of evidence that Ally had spent time earlier in the year with a man whose flashed identification bore a name and face that definitely matched Casey's former husband, Tim Thompson. It was always on Friday nights and never more than twice in a month. And while there were no eyewitnesses who'd gotten a good, close look at the man she'd been with, those who had spotted them together couldn't rule out that it was possibly Tim. In fact, the only thing—and it was a very small thing—in Tim's possible defense was that they hadn't managed to pull up any video surveillance providing concrete evidence that the man she was with was in fact him.

Finnick looked down at Joey. The child's big eyes were fixed seriously on his face.

Lord, I know that this is not the answer Casey wanted to hear. But if Tim truly is alive and fathered the tiny boy in my arms, please give me the evidence I need to bring him to justice.

Regardless of the cost.

Joey drained the bottle. The sound of children's voices singing filled the air outside the window. He looked out. Drew, Jessica and their three little girls were caroling outside the front door, in matching Christmas sweaters and hats. Casey leaned over the table and followed his gaze.

An uncomfortable and almost pained

look flickered in her eyes, and he was again reminded of how hard it must be for her to see Drew go on with his life, get married and have a perfect family while she'd felt her own life had stopped the day Drew's former fiancée and her former husband had vanished together. But then she blinked the look away, forced a smile and reached for Joey.

"Come on," she said to the infant brightly. "Let's go listen to the carolers."

She danced into the other room with Joey in her arms and opened the door. Nippy trotted after them and wagged his tail at the visitors.

"Merry Christmas Eve!" Casey said, with a cheerful tone that he suspected was directed at the three little girls. "What wonderful sweaters you're wearing!"

"Ooh, can I hold the baby?" The oldest girl's voice floated in through the open door. Her name was Sophie, if he remembered correctly. "I'll be really gentle and I won't drop him."

"She is really responsible," Jessica said. "She's going to be Mary in the nativity play today."

"No, I'm sorry," Casey said. "He's still getting used to strangers. But your singing was really lovely."

Finnick's phone began to ring. It was Gemma. He stepped away from the table, held the phone to his ear and pressed a finger to the other ear to block out the noise.

"Hey, boss," Gemma said. "So, you got the package of information we sent on the investigation?"

"Yeah." Finnick sighed. "I know that Casey's convinced that Tim is dead, but I've issued arrest warrants based on way less evidence than this, and we've probably got more than enough to get a court to approve it." He glanced from the window to the clock. "I'm not going to be able to get this before a judge until after Christmas. So we've got two days, whether we want them or not. Before I leave, I'm going to talk to Casey and see if we can get her to cooperate."

"Will she?"

"I hope so," Finnick said. "But I honestly don't know."

Lord, please prepare Casey's heart for this conversation and my own heart, for whatever her reaction happens to be.

He looked back out the window. The family had started singing again.

"I might be out of cell phone range for a bit on and off today," Gemma said, "Jackson and I are trying to do some last-minute things for Christmas, and you know what the cell signal is like on the rural roads."

"Yeah," Finnick said. He watched out the window as Drew pointed to the white-berried garland he'd hung up and made some kind of joke about it. He hadn't thought his decorating was that bad. "I know it's Christmas Eve and I promised I'd be there for the big team dinner, but even when the road reopens, I don't know how long it's going to take to get my van fixed and head out of here."

"Well, we're all looking forward to seeing you and Nippy."

"I'm looking forward to seeing you all too."

He ended the call as Casey thanked the carolers and closed the door. He stood in the doorway between the kitchen and living room, and watched as Casey laid Joey down on the play mat. Nippy took up his usual post on the carpet beside him with his nose on his paws.

"They're just going door to door to remind people about the nativity play," she said. Her cheeks were rosy from the cold air, and although a smile crossed her lips when she looked down at Joey, in the depths of her eyes he could see the echo of an old pain battling the current joy she felt as she looked up at him.

And Finnick wished with all his heart that he knew how to take that pain away.

"Did they happen to mention anything

about the break-in at Craft and Son Construction?" Finnick asked. "I imagine a construction van smashing through the park's Christmas display and crashing through the ice into the lake must be pretty big island gossip."

"Molly, the youngest one, asked me if I've heard that a thief stole Uncle Patrick's van and crashed through the lights—"

"Uncle Patrick?"

"They're not actually related," Casey explained, "just Drew and Patrick have always been close, and Patrick never moved on after Tristan's mother left. Anyway, Jessica cut her off before she could get to the part about it sinking in the lake and steered the conversation back to how important it is that everybody comes to the nativity play because we all have to do our part if Juniper Cove is going to win the Most Whimsical Christmas Village competition."

"I'd almost forgotten about that," Finnick said. "Okay, so what am I missing about this garland?" He reached up and tugged on it. "First, you made a weird face at it, then I saw Drew pointing at it."

"Oh." Casey laughed. She straightened up and turned to face him. "That's mistletoe."

"Mistletoe?" The word rang a very old bell in the back of his mind, but for a moment he couldn't place why. "It's poisonous, right?"

"Well, maybe in nature, but those berries are plastic." She shook her head and her laughter grew. "There's an old tradition about kissing someone who's standing under the mistletoe."

Heat rose to his face.

"Oh!" Of course, he should've known that. How had that slipped his mind? "I'm sorry. I didn't mean anything by it..."

"It's okay," Casey said, softly. Her hand brushed his arm. "I know you didn't and that's why I found it funny. You're really sweet and I'm so glad you're here."

Then she stood up on her tiptoes, leaned

toward him and brushed her lips against his cheek. Finnick startled and instinctively turned toward her. His lips accidentally brushed hers. Her fingers tightened on his arm. His hand reached around her back and pulled her closer.

And suddenly, Finnick found himself kissing her.

Casey was kissing Finnick.

For over a decade, she'd never imagined a man like Finnick would want to kiss someone like her. Not after her life had been turned inside out and torn apart. But now, years after first holding his hand, and hours after tumbling into his arms while chopping down a tree, Casey was being kissed by the most incredible, intelligent, kind and handsome man she knew.

She was kissing him back. His second hand wrapped around her waist and pulled her closer. Her fingers slid up into his hair.

The phone in the kitchen began to ring, with a loud jangling clatter, shattering the moment. She leaped back; so did Finnick, and for a moment, they just stared at each other, the surprise in his face mirroring the shock in her own heart. Her heart beat so hard in her chest she could barely breathe. What had she been thinking? Why had she kissed him?

Why had he kissed her?

The phone rang again. Casey stumbled another step back and mumbled a string of syllables that she intended to sound like an apology—not that she was exactly sure what she was apologizing for. Then she rushed into the kitchen to answer the phone. As she reached for it, she realized her hand was shaking.

"Hello," Casey said.

"Casey, I'm glad I caught you." It was the social worker. She sounded almost breathless with relief. "I have some really big and unexpected news about baby Joey."

"Oh, really?"

From the living room, Casey could hear Joey beginning to cry.

"It's okay!" Finnick called. "I've got him."

"As you know, a lot of these stories are pretty tragic," the social worker went on, "especially, in this case, after what happened to Joey's mother. It's not often I'm able to call someone with good news like this, but although I have to keep the specific details confidential for now, as the family wants us to wait until they make it public, we've found Joey's family and he's going home."

"Oh." Casey sank down into a chair, feeling like the balloon of joy that had been building in her core when Finnick kissed her, had suddenly popped.

"Are you okay?" Finnick asked, gently from the doorway. Worry filled his eyes.

She nodded. Of course it was wonderful news that Joey was going to be adopted. Usually the process took months, or even years. While Joey finding a permanent home had crushed the tiny flicker of hope—which Casey hadn't even admitted to herself she felt—that one day the little child would be hers, she also knew the adoption waiting list in Canada was so long, it was almost impossible that he'd ever be her son. The child's big eyes fixed on hers.

"I don't understand how you found an adoptive home for him so quickly," Casey said.

"No," the social worker said, "we found his father."

Casey suddenly felt lightheaded.

"You found Joey's father?" Casey echoed. "How?"

She could hear Finnick exhale a hard breath, but she didn't let herself turn and look at him.

"He contacted us," the social worker explained. "Apparently, he already has a family. It had been a brief relationship and Ally hadn't told him about the child. But when he heard about her death, he contacted social services right away. Of course, when the bridge reopens, he'll be coming here to sort some formalities, and he'll have to provide evidence to establish paternity. But we're hoping Joey will be home for Christmas."

Hot tears of relief, joy and sadness mingled together in her eyes, but she refused to let them fall. This was good news and she would thank God for it. The social worker's happy words were still spinning past her ear, when something she'd said finally caught up with Casey's brain.

"Why would Joey's father have to wait until the bridge reopens to establish paternity?" Casey asked. She watched as Finnick's eyes widened.

"Oh," the social worker said, "Joey's father lives on the island. He said he's hoping to make it to the Christmas event in Juniper Cove today, and if so, he's going to try to meet you and Joey. But again, that's up to him. I can't tell you anything about him or his family until everything's confirmed."

Casey nodded. "I understand."

"And of course, I'll head your way an hour or two after the bridge reopens and the traffic clears," the social worker added. "Apparently, people have camped out overnight to be first to cross over."

No doubt in a hurry to get home and see loved ones.

"Well, thank you so much for letting me know," Casey said. "I look forward to seeing you in a bit."

The call ended soon afterward, Casey hung up the phone and sat there for a long moment, staring at it, like it was a grenade about to go off.

"What was that about?" Finnick's voice sounded behind her.

"Joey's father has contacted social services to claim him," Casey said. She stood and turned toward him. Finnick's face was awash with compassion, maybe even worry.

"Are you okay?" Finnick asked.

He slid Joey into the crook of one arm and extended the other hand to her, in the silent offer of a hug. But if she let herself fall into his arms now, she was probably going to start crying and not even know why. So instead, she crossed her arms and he pulled his hand back.

"I'm fine," Casey said. She tried to force a smile and failed. "I'm just a bit surprised and overwhelmed. Apparently, Joey and his family live here on the island."

"Here?" Finnick repeated.

"Apparently," Casey repeated. "But it's good news, all around. Once social services get the details sorted out, Joey will be going home. And since he'll be here on this island, I might be able to get to know his family and watch him grow up. I don't know his father's name, but I'm sure you'll be able to get it once he meets with social services, and then your team will finally have a very solid lead they can chase to find out how Ally was killed.

Maybe he even knows who could've killed the mother of his child and who's been dressing up as the Creepy Shepherd."

She gasped a deep breath, not sure why the center of her chest was aching. Finnick didn't answer and the silence that had always seemed so comfortable before now felt painful.

"I mean, I suppose it's possible Joey's father is the Creepy Shepherd," she added after a long moment. "But that doesn't make any sense. Why hide your face, run around trying to snatch Joey away from us, and then walk into social services and admit you're Joey's dad? It doesn't make sense."

"I don't know," Finnick admitted. Something seemed to catch in his throat and he swallowed hard to clear it. "But once I know his name, I'll look into him and do everything I can to make sure he's a good dad for Joey. I promise, I'll do my best to keep him safe."

Casey swallowed too. "I know."

The next few hours passed much the same way as their lazy hours together had the day before. She played with Joey, fed him, put him down for a nap and got him back up again.

Finnick spent hours typing away on his computer, as well as talking to Rupert and trying to call members of his team, who were apparently traveling and out of service range. Unfortunately, there'd been no DNA found in the van once it was pulled from the river and Rupert's interview with Patrick had yielded no useful information.

Casey and Finnick shared a simple and cozy lunch together, which had been cobbled together with things she'd bought at the Christmas market. She hung the last few Christmas decorations, careful not to let her eyes wander to the mistletoe still hanging above the kitchen doorway, or her mind to the memory of the confusing and unwise kiss that still lingered on her lips. But even as they went through all the motions, the hours stretched out like a hollow echo of the time they'd spent together in the same farmhouse the day before, as the constant ticking of the clock reminded her that each bottle she fed Joey, each scratch she gave Nippy behind the ears and each unexpected glance she shared with Finnick brought her closer to her last.

Shortly after lunch, Casey was down on the carpet playing with Joey when the faint sound of church bells filled the frosty air outside her windows. She looked up to where Finnick sat at the kitchen table.

"It's time for the nativity pageant," she said.

He closed his laptop. "You want to go?"

No, she didn't. But did that matter?

"Eileen will be pretty disappointed if I don't." Casey got up slowly and stretched. "Plus, it might be your best opportunity to find out who Joey's biological father is, if he happens to be there."

At least if another man stepped forward and proved that he was Joey's father, it would also prove that it wasn't Tim.

Not that it would prove Tim wasn't alive, and that he hadn't killed Stella or Ally.

She looked out the window, and to her surprise saw just as many cars driving away from Juniper Cove as there were driving toward it. Eileen wasn't going to like that. She was counting on a full house for the nativity play and had messaged Casey three times that morning to double-check she was coming.

Casey glanced back. "Has the bridge reopened? People are driving out of town."

Finnick checked his phone.

"It's almost open," he said. "I guess they're going to join the line. The van is cleared, the repairs are done and they're just doing a safety inspection now. They expect traffic will be able to leave the island in less than two hours, and then once that backlog is cleared, the bridge will open the other direction for people to cross onto the island." A small smile crossed his lips. "It's almost over."

She smiled back weakly. They drove

to Juniper Cove Community Church in Casey's van, each in the same position they'd been in the night before during their terrifying vehicle chase, with Casey at the wheel, Finnick in the passenger seat and Nippy curled up in the back with a watchful eye over Joey in the car seat.

She'd been expecting to see yellow police tape up in front of the park where the van had crashed. But to her surprise, any tape that had been strung up had been taken down and the dancing penguins were back up, with only the mess of tire tracks and broken branches as evidence of the van that crashed through the area last night.

"I'd no idea police could clean up a scene this fast," Casey said.

"Well, I got the impression from Rupert that your sister put a lot of pressure on them to get the lights back up," Finnick said. His eyes scanned the whimsical holiday world outside his window. "The competition closes tomorrow morning and she thought it was important Juniper Cove put its best foot forward."

Then he sighed.

"What's up?" Casey asked, as she eased the car into a parallel parking spot on the busy street.

"Last night," he said, "as I was walking through town, before Nippy alerted to the van and everything kicked off, I was thinking about the fact that for years I never really attended Christmas events like this. Because each year I made a point of volunteering for the skeleton crew who worked over the holidays so that other officers could be home with their families. Most years I didn't even have a tree, besides the little six-inch one I put on my table at home and the big one I authorized for the whole K-9 department. Usually the only gift I bought and wrapped was for Nippy. Besides that, I just made a personal donation to charity on behalf of my coworkers and gave out some gift cards to the cleaning and cafeteria staff who were stuck working the holiday with me."

She cut the engine but didn't reach for the door handle. Instead, she turned and looked at Finnick.

"But I never once felt like I was missing out on Christmas," he went on, "even those years that Nippy and I spent at crime scenes, and I was too run off my feet to even eat one of the gingerbread doughnuts in the cafeteria. The knowledge that an all-powerful, loving God had decided to come down to Earth felt closer to me when we were tracking a scent through frozen swamps in sludge up to my knees than it does here, surrounded by all this Christmassy stuff."

Finnick waved his arms in both directions, gesturing at the lights and decorations around them. Then he sighed and ran one hand through his graying hair.

"All of this is really incredible and lovely," he went on, and Casey realized it was probably the most she'd ever heard him talk. "I don't mean to imply I think there's anything wrong with it. It gives people joy and brings the community together. And it's clear people put a lot of hard work into it. I just hope that at the same time, people remember there is more to Christmas than all this, even if they find it in a very different way than I do."

Again, his hand floated in the empty space between them, and again, she was tempted to take it but didn't.

"I hope so too," she said.

Finnick instructed Nippy to stay in the car and left the back window cracked wide enough that the old fellow could get out if he needed to. Then Finnick and Casey headed inside, with Joey in Casey's arms. The church was packed with extra folding chairs, squeezed in at the edges of the pews. Despite the traffic she'd seen heading toward the bridge earlier, it looked like people had come from across the island to watch the nativity play.

There were maybe three hundred people in the room, she guessed, more than five times the usual number they had at a Sunday service. Presumably at least one of the people there was an undercover judge who'd come to judge the competition as well, assuming they'd made it to the island before the bridge was closed. It was funny to think the whole competition could be going on with nobody there to actually judge it.

Casey scanned the crowd. Over a third of the attendees were men—young men, family men and newlyweds. Was Joey's father in the room somewhere? If so, would he come up and introduce himself?

They found two seats near the back, on the aisle, squeezed in and watched as Eileen ran around the stage, organizing kids in long robes and animal costumes, while Pastor David coordinated the choir. Cameron moved silently, like a shadow, at the edge of the room, taking candid pictures. A large stack of song sheets were passed from person to person, down the rows.

Pastor David asked everyone to kindly put their cell phones away for now, and that he'd let them know when they were free to get their cameras back out and take pictures during the final carol. Then finally, when Eileen had ushered a final child back behind a curtain, and Cameron had disappeared along with them, Pastor David gestured everyone to their feet, the choir started and everyone began to sing.

Casey bounced the baby in her arms and Finnick held one song sheet between them so they could share it. His shoulder brushed against hers. Music swelled, filling the room and surrounding them on all sides, and despite the pain and uncertainty, she felt an unexpected burst of joy spreading through her heart. Her whole life, she'd never seen this many people from across the island for a Christmas play and if a competition was what it took to bring people together, then she was thankful for it. She scanned the room, then her gaze drifted to the beautiful snow outside the window.

And she gasped.

A man in the Creepy Shepherd mask and robes was watching them through the glass.

EIGHT

Finnick heard Casey inhale sharply and felt her hand grasp his arm.

"What?" He leaned toward her, so they could speak in the room filled with music, until their faces were so close they almost touched. As her eyes met his, fear filled their depths.

"The Creepy Shepherd is outside," she said, "watching through the window."

Finnick turned and looked behind him, past the throngs of carolers singing to the window where she was gesturing. For a moment, all he saw was the snowy landscape and bright blue sky. If it had been any civilian other than Casey, he might have questioned if she was seeing something. After all, why would the Creepy

Shepherd take the risk of looking into a public space in broad daylight? It didn't make sense. But he'd worry about that later. All that mattered now was stopping him.

He strained his eyes, searching the endless white outside and prayed.

Lord, guide my vision and help me see.

Then, out of the corner of his eye, he saw a flash of green disappear over a snowbank to their right and vanish out of sight. He took Casey's hand and squeezed it.

"I'm going after him," Finnick said. "Stay here, surrounded by people. Don't go anywhere alone or leave until I come back for you. Got it?"

Casey nodded. "Got it."

He allowed himself one more look at her face, wishing he didn't have to leave her and praying today was the day he finally brought the criminal who'd been terrorizing her to justice. Then he set his jaw in determination. "I won't let him get away this time."

Finnick slid past her into the aisle and made his way to the back of the church as quickly as he could without actually breaking into a run. That would wait until he was outside. He reached the front steps and sprinted for Casey's van.

"Nippy!" he called as he ran toward his partner. The K-9 woofed loudly, leaped through the window, hit the frozen ground and bounded down the sidewalk toward Finnick. Within a heartbeat, Nippy was by his side. Together as one, Finnick and his partner turned and dashed down a narrow alley between two buildings and came out in a large, snowy field behind the church. The Creepy Shepherd was nowhere to be seen, but a trail of footprints on the ground led over a hill down into the park.

Finnick and Nippy raced ahead, chasing the trail of footprints through the snow. The park spread out before them in a maze of trees, benches, children's playground equipment and light displays, set in a natural valley with hills on three sides. The figure in the green robe weaved his way through the trees.

"Stop!" Finnick shouted. His hand flexed toward the badge on his waist, but once again, he didn't pull it. The man wouldn't even be able to see it from this distance. Even if he did, Finnick had no reason to believe he'd halt, and he'd just have given up the element of surprise.

The Creepy Shepherd glanced back but didn't stop. Finnick pressed his legs faster than he'd even dared when he was a young man. The old dog beside him matched him pace for pace. The Creepy Shepherd had a pretty good head start. But Finnick had the high ground and he wasn't in a ridiculous disguise.

But did the criminal still have a gun? And if so, would he shoot to kill a dog? Finnick swallowed hard and glanced at his faithful partner running beside him. He hated to put Nippy in danger. But it was what the dog had trained for in the line of duty and the retriever was still a cop, through and through.

Lord, please give me wisdom and keep Nippy safe.

Finnick took a breath and made the call.

"Chase him!" he ordered, pointing at the figure in the Creepy Shepherd robes. "Go!"

Nippy barked like a warrior and ran straight down the slope toward the figure. Finnick darted sharply upward and ran along the top of the hill to his left, weaving behind trees and hoping with each step that the Creepy Shepherd would be too focused on the loud dog charging behind him to even notice Finnick gaining on him.

The shepherd seemed leaner than he'd been the night before. Was that the trick of the light? Or someone new beneath the mask? The shepherd glanced back again and almost stumbled as he saw the dog charging down the hill after him. Then he reached into his robes. Something reflective flashed in his hand.

It was now or never.

Finnick leaped, throwing himself down the embankment like a linebacker, tackling the Creepy Shepherd around the shoulders and throwing him down onto the ground. The assailant shouted in surprise, but his words were muffled as he fell. The object flew from the Shepherd's hand and landed in the snow. It wasn't a gun. It was a cell phone and according to the screen notification a message had just been sent.

"Stay down!" Finnick pinned the guy face down in the snow. "Hands where I can see them and don't try anything."

Nippy leaped to his side. The dog was still barking fiercely, but Finnick signaled the dog to stop. Then he flipped the man over and yanked the mask up, and saw the young, terrified face of Patrick's twelve-year-old-son.

This was no criminal killer. This was a very young man, barely out of childhood.

"Tristan?" Finnick leaped up off the kid, feeling his own head jerk back in surprise. "I'm sorry, I didn't mean to scare you. What are you doing running around in that costume? Who gave it to you and made you do this? Was it your dad?"

The kid's mouth opened and then shut again, like a caught fish gasping for air. Finnick reached down to help Tristan to his feet. But instead of taking his hand, Tristan's eyes darted over Finnick's shoulder and Finnick heard the sound of someone churning up the snow as they ran toward him.

"Leave my son alone!" a voice bellowed.

Finnick spun back. Patrick was charging down the hill toward him. The father's face was flushed with anger. The contractor was a good decade and a half younger than Finnick, a couple inches taller and fueled by the indignant rage of seeing someone lay a hand on his child.

And even though Finnick was certain he'd be able to hold his own against him in a fight, and eventually wrestle him down, he'd probably take a few painful blows in the process—and more importantly lose any hope of getting a real answer out of him. Patrick's fist was clenched in rage. It rose, ready to strike.

Well, if it had to come to blows, Finnick wasn't going to throw down first.

Even if it turned out that Tristan had gotten the Creepy Shepherd costume from his own father, and that Patrick himself was somehow behind all this, Finnick was going to try his best to resolve it calmly, without fighting the man in front of his son.

"Hey, it's okay," Finnick said. He raised his right hand, palm open to show that he was unarmed, and with the left hand, he flashed his badge inside his jacket, making a point to hide it from Tristan's view. "Your son is fine and I don't want trouble. I just need his help and yours."

Tristan scrambled to his feet, yanked off the mask and threw it in the snow. Patrick stopped just a few feet away from Finnick and close enough to strike. His arms didn't drop. Patrick's eyes darted rapid fire from the badge, to his son, to Finnick's face and then back to Tristan's face again. Nippy stepped to Finnick's side.

"Tristan," Patrick called to his son. His voice was protective, but serious too. "Are you okay?"

Tristan nodded. "Yeah, yeah."

"Son, just tell me the truth," Patrick said, "and it's going to be okay."

"I was running," Tristan began, and then his words poured out in one nonstop thought, "and he ran after me, and he yelled at me to stop, and I didn't because I knew I'd be in trouble for taking this costume, and then he tackled me and I fell down, and I'm okay because it's my fault."

"No, it's my fault, Tristan," Finnick said, quickly. "I thought you were someone else. A very dangerous man, who attacked a friend of mine while wearing that costume. If I'd known it was you, I wouldn't have chased you like that. I'd have gone and found your dad."

Patrick hesitated a moment, as if weighing Finnick's words and trying to decide whether he believed them. Then he blew out a loud breath and ran both hands over his head.

"Take it off, Tristan," Patrick said. "Where did you get it?"

"It was in the church storage room with the nativity costumes." Tristan wriggled out of the robe and held it out to his father. But when Patrick didn't take it, he turned to Finnick.

"You can put it in the snow with the mask. That's fine," Finnick said.

"None of the older kids wanted to be in the pageant," Tristan said. The boy folded the robe awkwardly and then dropped it on top of the mask. "But Mrs. Wilks was saying we all have to. Then, when we were getting ready, we found this and everyone said it would be funny if somebody put it on and ran around. And so I did."

The kid squirmed. Nippy walked over to Tristan, with his ears low and tail wagging, and butted his head against the boy's leg. Tristan glanced to his dad as if for permission.

"Nippy's a good dog," Finnick said. "He's really good with kids."

Patrick nodded to Tristan. The boy ran his hand over the dog's head.

"Do you know whose idea it first was that somebody run around in the costume?" Finnick asked.

Tristan shook his head.

"Do you know how the mask and robe got into the storage room?" Finnick added.

Tristan shook his head again. Finnick took in a long breath and let it out.

"Okay, how about you and Nippy go sit on that bench over there—" Finnick pointed to a snow-covered bench a few yards away "—while I have a talk with your dad."

Once again, Tristan looked to his dad for agreement.

"Yeah," Patrick agreed, "and put your headphones on okay? Because Mr. Ethan and I might have some things to talk about, which I don't want you to have to worry about."

Patrick reached out a gloved hand to his son, and Tristan gave him a fist-bump. Finnick signaled to Nippy to go with the boy, and Tristan and Nippy headed over to the bench. Finnick waved Patrick to a different seat, where they sat side by side. The boy and dog began to play in the snow, despite Tristan having just been told to sit on the bench.

Patrick shook his head at his son and grinned.

"You've got a really great kid," Finnick said.

"I know." Patrick sighed. He sounded both tired and frustrated. "Though I don't know what I ever did to deserve a son that great. Is that a police dog?"

"Yeah," Finnick said. "Although, he's technically retired."

"What's his specialty?"

"Cadaver."

"Wow." Patrick blew out another breath and dropped his head into his hands. "Look, I know why you're here and I've got nothing new to tell you. I didn't kill Stella or Tim. I didn't touch that other girl. And I've got plenty of home security footage proving I didn't leave my house last night, let alone break into my own construction yard and run over my own gate. But I know you guys have already made your mind up about me. So just tell me what I need to do to get you to stop harassing me."

"Well, I'm not here to harass you," Finnick said, "I just got here, and I can promise you, I definitely haven't made my mind up about you." Patrick pulled his hands away from his face and looked at him. Finnick stuck out his hand as if to shake his. "I'm Inspector Ethan Finnick, formerly head of the Ontario RCMP's K-9 Unit, soon to be head of the newly formed Cold Case Task Force."

Patrick looked at his hand and didn't take it. But something seemed to soften in his eyes. "So, you're here about Stella and Tim?"

"Yup," Finnick said, "and I'm also trying to figure out why a man in a shepherd costume broke into your lot, attacked Casey, tried to steal the infant who was left in her nativity manger and used one of your old vehicles to potentially kidnap a woman named Ally Neilson, kill her and dispose of her body."

"Well, it wasn't me," Patrick said.

"I do imagine that if you were going to use one of your vans to commit a crime you'd probably choose one with decent snow tires," Finnick said.

Patrick snorted, and for the first time since he'd come running across the snow, the man actually managed a smile. "I'm sure Casey thinks I have something to do with what happened to Tim and Stella."

She does, Finnick thought. But that didn't mean she was right.

"Why do you say that?" Finnick asked.

"Because everybody blamed me for what happened," Patrick said, "because I apparently saw them last. Even though I heard that someone saw them in Sudbury weeks later."

"Do you know who started that rumor that they were seen in Sudbury?" Finnick asked. "Or who supposedly saw them there?"

"No." Patrick shook his head, but Finnick wasn't so sure he didn't at least have some idea, even if it was just a guess. "I was brought in for questioning and declared a 'person of interest.' But I have never officially been cleared."

"Because the case was never closed."

"Right," Patrick said, "and people don't care about the difference between a suspect and a person of interest. I already had a reputation because of Tristan and his mom."

His voice dropped, as if worrying Tristan might overhear him.

"The only thing I'm guilty of is having a kid with a chick who didn't want to marry me, when I was too young to be having a family," Patrick went on. "When Tristan was born, I dropped out of college, started working for my dad full time, and made being Tristan's dad my highest priority. But his mom only wanted to go out, drink and party. She didn't want to settle down and was dating other guys behind my back. Eventually, she left us and we haven't heard from her in years. But, of course, people assumed it was my fault and that I'd done something wrong."

"And you never tried to move on?" Finnick asked.

"It's kind of hard to move on when any woman who researches me online for more than five minutes discovers I'm a person of interest in what looks like a double homicide." Patrick didn't even try to hide the resentment in his voice. But again something softened in his eyes when he glanced at his son, who was now wrestling with Nippy in the snow. "Tristan's an amazing kid and I'm really blessed that I get to be his dad. So what if no one on this island believes me when I say I've never so much as touched a drink in my life, and that I really wanted to marry Tristan's mom? But, I had a child out of wedlock. That was all the reason people needed to think badly of me. And so people are going to believe what they're going to believe, whether it's true or not."

"Not if I can help it," Finnick said.

But Patrick went on as if he hadn't heard him. "And everyone seems to think I might be guilty of something."

Casey had said everyone thought Tim was guilty of something. Rupert had said the same about Stella. And now Patrick was saying the same about himself. It seemed there was more than enough finger pointing and blame throwing to go around.

So, all three of them had been blamed. Did that mean none of them were guilty?

He glanced back at the church where he'd left Casey and Joey. The faint sound of singing still echoed in the air.

Lord, give me clarity. It feels like no one is telling me the whole truth about anything to do with this case—maybe because none of them know it.

Give me eyes to see the truth.

No matter where it leads.

Casey bounced Joey on her lap and watched as Sophie shuffled slowly down the aisle, enveloped in a beautiful pale blue robe with a white-lined blue scarf over her head. She walked between a Joseph with a full false beard and wooden staff on one side and a child dressed as a soft gray donkey on the other.

Up onstage almost two dozen children from Juniper Cove and around the island posed in a tableau of angels, shepherds, wise men and sheep. Every craftsperson in town who'd been able to wield a sewing needle, glue gun, hammer or paint brush had donated their time to work on the costumes and sets. The final impact of it all coming together was spectacular, and despite the constant thrum of worry in Casey's heart as she kept scanning the windows and entrance for Finnick, she was also incredibly happy for her sister and what she'd managed to create.

Eileen had not only put together something truly spectacular, she'd managed to bring the whole town, and even the island, together in a way it never had before.

Lord, thank You for my sister's gifts and determination, for what she's been able to put together for our town. Whether we win this competition or not, please use this Christmas to strengthen our community and bring people closer to each other and to You.

And please, bring Finnick back soon and keep him and Nippy safe.

Mary, Joseph and the donkey reached the stage. Pastor David invited everyone to stand and sing "Silent Night," and announced that those with children, grandchildren and loved ones up onstage were welcome to get their cameras out again and start taking pictures. Cameron stepped in the center aisle and knelt down to take pictures of the pageant.

Joey began to fuss and complain that he was ready for a fresh bottle and a nap, when suddenly Casey realized that something was going wrong onstage, in the center of the nativity scene. Sophie was searching around the manger as if looking for something she couldn't find. Soon, Joseph, a couple of shepherds and the angel Gabriel were helping her, looking under hay bales and glancing to their parents with increasingly distressed looks on their faces. A young angel said something to Eileen in a voice too low for Casey to catch, and from the way her sister's smile tightened, Casey knew immediately that something was wrong.

The children seemed to be getting more confused and frazzled.

But it wasn't until the song came to an end that Sophie's voice finally reached Casey's ears.

"I've looked everywhere and can't find it!" The frustrated girl's voice rose. "Baby Jesus is gone!"

A buzz spread through the crowd, and suddenly the beautiful harmony that had filled the room just moments before had been replaced with whispers, murmurs and even a few snickers. A few parents left their seats to help look for the doll. Smaller children started to wander around the stage. A couple of the more enthusiastic ones began to search more aggressively. And a few of the older teenagers in the audience switched their camera to video mode and started to crack jokes about the final act of the pageant unraveling in front of them.

Some people enjoyed watching other people's tragedies.

There in the middle of the hurricane was her sister Eileen, trying to do everything at once, shooing children back to their places and waving the parents to stay in their seats, while also searching every possible onstage hiding place for the missing doll.

Then through the crowd, Casey felt Drew's eyes on her. As she watched, he leaned over to Jessica and murmured something to her. Jessica slipped quietly to the center of the chaos and whispered to Eileen. Eileen turned and looked straight at Casey, and the baby in her arms.

And Casey felt the tiniest bit of dread begin to drip down inside her core.

Eileen went to the podium, picked up a portable microphone, turned to the congregation and smiled.

"Everybody back in your seats, please,"

she said. "Kids, let's all get back in position. It's picture time."

People began to settle, kids returned to formation, and even the teenagers who'd been on their phones lowered them and stopped talking.

"I know we are all a little bit surprised by the fact that the baby Jesus doll we practiced with has gone missing," Eileen started, in her best Sunday-school voice, smiling at the kids and the congregation. "Sometimes, things happen that we don't expect, especially at Christmas. My little sister, Casey, got a huge Christmas surprise this week, when a little tiny baby boy showed up in the manger outside her house, needing a place to stay. Thankfully, Casey took him in and kept him safe."

People were turning to face Casey now as Eileen walked down the aisle toward her. A couple of people actually snapped a picture of her and Joey, and Casey couldn't remember ever seeing that many people smiling at her at once.

Casey's breath tightened in her chest and she instinctively hugged Joey closer to her. He nestled into her chest and whimpered softly.

She never wanted to let her sister down. She never wanted to let anybody down.

Let alone while her sister was putting her on the spot, in front of everyone.

Casey's words to Finnick the day before echoed in her mind.

She's impossible to say no to, which is why I never do.

Well, I'll be the one saying no to her, not you.

Casey glanced at the doorway.

Where was Finnick?

Lord, please don't let Eileen ask me something I have to say no to.

"Now, Joey is a very little and very special baby," Eileen said, still holding the mic, "and it's important that we take care of him. But we're going to have a real live baby in the manger this year, not just a doll. Because Casey has agreed that if Sophie is very careful, she can hold Joey for a few quick pictures, to welcome him as a part of the Juniper Cove family Christmas."

There was a smattering of applause. Eileen leaned toward Casey and stretched out her hands. Casey took a painful breath.

"No," she said. Eileen's eyes widened as if Casey had physically pushed her. "I'm sorry. But Joey can't be in the nativity scene."

"But I was told you talked to Sophie earlier, and said you were okay with it."

The microphone was still amplifying her voice.

"Well, I'm sorry," Casey said, again. "But she must've misunderstood. Joey's too little and I'm only his temporary guardian. His father has already contacted social services and is hoping to take him home by Christmas, and he might not want him appearing in pictures for a holiday competition."

Was his father even there? Or any members of his family?

If so, why didn't they step in?

Or was he watching her for some reason? And if so, what was he watching her for?

Something sharp flickered in her sister's eyes.

Anger? Pain?

Humiliation?

Then she saw Cameron step up behind his mother. His worried eyes met Casey's and he shook his head.

"Stop it," Eileen hissed. "You're making a scene and embarrassing both of us. This nativity pageant is a really important part of the contest and we can't have nativity pictures with no baby Jesus. It's only going to be for a couple of minutes and then you can have him back."

Joey began to cry, for no other reason, Casey suspected, than he was getting more tired and hungry. But Eileen's lips pursed.

"Look, now you're upsetting him, Casey," she said. "Just let me hold him and I promise we'll just get some pictures and then it'll all be done."

"She said no, Mom," Cameron said. He placed his hand gently on his mother's arm. "It was a good idea, but Casey's got a point. Just let it go and we'll wrap up a towel or something for the pictures."

"Cameron, stop." Eileen turned to her son. "It's fine. I've got it. Stay out of it."

"Mom, he's a kid," Cameron said. "Not a prop for your show."

Casey wasn't sure what drew her eyes past her sister and nephew to the doorway. Was it a sound? A motion? But whatever it was, Finnick was now there. His eyes met hers and he smiled. Her heart leaped.

"I'm so sorry," she said loudly to no one in particular. She slid past Eileen. "He needs me to change him and give him a bottle."

Voices and faces swam around her. She blocked them out, focusing her attention on Finnick. As she drew near, he reached out his hand for her, like she was drowning and he was offering to pull her to shore. She took it and together they hurried down the aisle and out the door.

"Are you okay?" Finnick asked her, softly.

"Yes," she said. "Maybe. I don't know. I might've just wrecked my sister's attempt to win the Christmas competition."

"I'm sure you didn't," Finnick said.

Nippy was waiting for them on the front step. His tail thumped hello.

"Are you okay?" she asked. "Where's the Creepy Shepherd?"

"It wasn't him," Finnick said. "It was Tristan. He said the kids found the costume in the storage room, and he decided to run around in it. I thought Patrick was going to deck me when he realized I'd tackled his kid. But we ended up having a pretty decent talk."

"Oh?" She jostled Joey in her arms but his cries didn't settle.

"I'll explain more when we're in the van."

They hurried down the sidewalk together, and that was when she realized that she still hadn't let go of his hand and he hadn't let go of hers either.

When they reached the van, Joey's fussing had turned to full-out wails.

"Is he okay?" Finnick had to raise his voice just to be heard over him.

"He's just hungry, tired and determined to let us know."

Finnick smiled slightly. "Good for you, kid."

She got in the back with Joey and let Finnick drive, with Nippy in the passenger seat. There was so much she wanted to talk to Finnick about, but Joey seemed to be trying out his lungs at full volume, and they were unable to get a word in edgewise.

When they got home, she was immediately swept up in a flurry of activity taking care of the baby. She changed him, fed him, bounced him and changed him again, while Finnick took phone calls and checked things on his laptop.

She'd been home for over an hour before she finally managed to settle Joey again and he fell asleep peacefully in his crib. She stood there by his side, looking down at the dozing baby, feeling happier and more exhausted than she'd ever remembered feeling before.

"I don't know how somebody so little and cute could make so much noise and trouble," she whispered softly, running a hand down his cheek. "But you're the most incredible kid and even though you're going to be leaving me soon, I'm going to think about you and pray for you every day of my life."

She blinked away tears and refused to let them fall. When Casey slipped out of the room, she could hear Finnick's voice floating down the hall. He was clearly on the phone with someone, probably Rupert. So instead she slipped into her bedroom, plugged her cell phone into the charger beside the bed, lay down on top of the blankets and stared at the wall of Thompson-family pictures facing the bed. The room had never really felt like hers. Instead, it was a memory capsule of all the families who'd lived on the Thompson farm before. There were pictures of Tim's great-grandparents and grandparents, great uncles and aunts, his parents, and Tim as a child. And there was an empty space where her and Tim's picture was supposed to go once they finally had kids of their own.

She closed her eyes, and finally, the tears she'd managed to fight before began to slip out from under her lids and slide down her cheeks. For a moment, she lay there and cried, without even understanding why, just knowing she had to take it to God.

"Lord," she whispered, "I don't know if I've been wrong all this time in thinking Tim did nothing wrong and he was dead.

Or if Tim really is alive and was having a relationship with Ally, or how that fits in with the fact that Joey's father has contacted social services. I feel... I feel like I don't really know anything right now. Am I wrong for hoping You want me to be a mother and have a family of my own? Was I wrong to get Tim declared legally dead so I could use his insurance money to save his family farm? It meant so much to him and I felt like I'd betray him if I lost the farm to strangers outside of his family. Should I help Finnick and his team get Tim's death overturned? And if I do, what happens then?"

She took a shuddering breath and suddenly she realized her palms were aching. She'd hadn't even realized her hands were clenched. But now she was aware of how tightly she was squeezing her fingers closed and pressing her fingernails into her skin.

Slowly, she released her hand. Then she stretched her palms up toward the sky, feeling the tension ease from her aching shoulders as she did so, and she wondered how long she'd hunched them.

"Well, I'm lost right now, Lord," she said, "and so all I can do is be open to You. Show me what comes next. And I'll follow."

The sound of Finnick's voice on the phone was still floating down the hall and the tears had dried on Casey's cheeks. So she curled up in a ball on top of the bed and let herself doze.

Sleep came easily and peacefully, enveloping her gently and draining the tension from her limbs. Until suddenly she awoke to the sound of her cell phone ringing. She glanced at the screen. It was just before five, but already the sky was dark outside.

"Hello?"

"Aunt Casey?" Cameron's voice was breathless and panicked. "I need your help."

She bolted upright, swung her legs over

the side of the bed and started for the door. A crash sounded down the line.

"Where are you?" she asked. "Are you okay?"

No answer. Just another crash. She flung the bedroom door open and ran down the hall. Finnick was sitting on the couch, but when he heard her coming, he leaped to his feet and started toward her.

"Cameron!" Her voice rose as she spoke into the phone again. "Where are you? What's happening?"

"I'm at home in the darkroom—" his voice dropped to a terrified whisper "—hiding from someone. One second."

The call went silent without ending, like he'd put it on mute. Finnick reached for her hand and pulled her to his side. She held the phone between them so he could listen in too. A cheerful gurgle suddenly broke through the silence. She looked down to see Joey smiling and waving at her from his play mat, and she realized Finnick must've gotten him up from his nap while she was sleeping. Nippy lay in his usual spot beside him. The dog's dark eyes were fixed on her, with his ears down, as if silently asking her what was wrong.

"He's wearing a black mask, clothes and gloves." Cameron's panicked voice was back. "He just broke in and started looking through drawers. I think he's searching for something I took."

"Like a picture?" she asked.

Had her nephew managed to snap a photograph of the Creepy Shepherd? Or who had left his costume in the church?

But any answer Cameron would've given was lost with the sound of a man shouting profanity and threatening to kill her nephew. Whatever the attacker was looking for, he sounded willing to trash Eileen and David's garage to find it.

"Cameron?" Casey called. "What did you take? Who does it belong to?"

"I'm sorry," Cameron said. "I should've told you before. Ally—"

Then the heart-wrenching sound of her nephew screaming filled the line.

And the phone went dead.

NINE

Finnick watched the color drain from Casey's face.

"Cameron!" she shouted again. "Are you okay?"

But there was no answer. Casey called back and the phone just rang, but Finnick was already throwing on his jacket and grabbing his boots.

"I'm on my way," Finnick said. "You coming or staying?"

While he hated the idea of letting Casey go into a dangerous situation, he also knew that if one of his loved ones was in trouble, he'd be beating down the door to help them. He also didn't like the idea of leaving her, in case this was some kind of a diversion to get Finnick to race over there and leave Casey home alone with Joey.

"I'm coming," Casey said. She gasped a breath. Her limbs were shaking. "But you'd better drive."

"Hey, it's going to be okay." Finnick touched her shoulders gently with both hands. "We're going to go save him."

She bundled herself and Joey up in winter clothes, and the four of them ran for the van. Finnick opened the back door for her, then once she and Joey were securely inside, he and Nippy leaped in the front and they set off. Finnick called the island police using the van's hand's-free system and they assured him that the police and ambulance were on their way but would be a good twenty minutes out. The sun was already setting and the sky was growing dark. Finnick navigated her van down the icy roads, driving as quickly as he dared.

Minutes ticked past agonizingly slowly. Casey kept dialing Cameron and got no response. No answer from her sister either, which wasn't a surprise as she'd be at the skating event.

Then Eileen and David's house came into view. The lights were off and the driveway was empty, but a two-foot gap of light shone under the partially opened garage door.

"You're going to stay in the van with Joey, okay?" Finnick said. "And at the first sign of trouble, I want you and Joey to get out of here. Don't worry about me."

"Okay."

He reached over the back seat to hand her the keys and their fingertips brushed. Casey closed her eyes and whispered, "Lord, please help."

"Amen," Finnick said.

Then he exited the van, signaled Nippy to his side and ran for the garage. Silence fell from within.

"Hello?" he called. "Is anybody there?"

No answer. Finnick grabbed the garage door, rolled it up and froze.

Cameron's lifeless body was hanging by a noose from a garage support beam.

Casey's nephew was dead.

Sadness crashed into Finnick's chest like a wave as he walked over and touched the man's wrist. No pulse. A van door clicked open behind him. Finnick spun back, about to remind her to stay in the van, but the words froze on his tongue when he saw the sorrow flooding her eyes. She'd opened the back door, stepped just one foot out, with her other foot still in the car.

"Casey, I'm so sorry. Please stay there. I'm going to cut him down—"

But before the words could finish leaving his mouth, he heard Nippy bark and felt the dog butt his head against his leg. He looked down. Nippy's worried eyes were on his face. But the dog wasn't alerting.

"Casey!" Finnick shouted. "Help!" He sprinted into the garage, grabbed Cameron's legs and hoisted him up. "Cameron's still alive!"

She leaped from the van, slammed the door shut behind her and ran to help him.

"I'll hold him," Finnick said. "Find something you can use to climb up and cut him down. Nippy, go sit by the van and guard Joey."

The dog woofed and ran to the vehicle. Desperate prayers poured from Casey's lips. She grabbed a knife from the tool bench. Then ran for a stepladder that had fallen over a few feet away. Casey set the ladder beside Finnick and climbed up.

"You got it?" he asked.

"Yeah." She gritted her teeth. "Just be prepared to catch him."

She made quick work of the rope, and Cameron's full weight fell into Finnick's arms. He eased the young man onto the ground and reached for the knife. Wordlessly, Casey jumped down and handed it to him. Finnick cut the rope free from Cameron's neck, then pulled off his gloves and slid his bare fingers over the young man's red and raw skin, and felt for a pulse again. He didn't seem to be breathing.

Please, Lord, may Nippy be right. May there still be hope.

Casey knelt on the floor beside him and began to pray. At first, Finnick felt nothing, and then, he felt the tiniest flicker of a beat under his fingertips.

"He has a pulse!" Finnick sat back. "It's very slow and weak, but it's there. Can you do chest compressions? I'm going to attempt CPR."

"Thank You, God." Casey's eyes snapped open.

He eased Cameron's mouth open and stopped. There were remnants of a white powder around his lips, in his mouth and a little on the collar of his shirt.

"I think whoever did this to him drugged him so he wouldn't fight back," Finnick said. "It would explain why I couldn't find a pulse."

Suddenly lights and sirens filled the air. Joey began to wail in complaint at the sudden burst of noise. Police and paramedics suddenly flooded the area.

"We need a paramedic!" Finnick shouted, as uniformed law enforcement ran toward him. "He's alive but unconscious, and he seems to have been drugged with something that sedated him."

He stepped away from Cameron and let medical staff rush past him and do their job. Casey ran back to the van and climbed in to comfort Joey. Rupert strode up to Finnick. Judging by the older man's Christmas-patterned pajama pants, he hadn't even stopped to change.

"Was this a suicide attempt?" the chief of the island police asked, glancing at the rope.

"No." Finnick shook his head. "But somebody went to an awful lot of trouble to make it look like one."

But why?

Finnick walked back to the van, opened the back door and reached for Casey's hand. She took it and squeezed it tightly.

And for a long moment, he stood there, holding her left hand while her right hand rested on Joey, praying silently as they watched the paramedics work.

"He stood up to his mom for me," Casey said, softly.

Finnick opened his eyes. "When?"

"At the nativity service." Her eyes were fixed on the cluster of people gathered around her nephew in the garage. He watched as the flashing lights sent colorful shadows dancing down the lines of her face. "The whole thing was going perfectly, until nobody could find the baby Jesus doll. Then Eileen announced to everyone that we were going to have a real live baby in the manger because I was going to let Sophie hold Joey just for the pictures. I think Jessica put her up to it. Maybe in their attempt to get the next perfect picture for their family Christmas card. I don't know. The whole thing felt really manipulative. Eileen put me on the spot in front of everyone."

"And you said no?" Finnick asked.

"I did," Casey said. "Eileen didn't want to take no for an answer, and then Cameron stepped in and defended me. He basically told his mother off. It was a big scene and there's nothing Eileen hates more than a scene. I tried calling her and David when you were talking to law enforcement but couldn't get through."

"And the whole town saw it," Finnick said.

"Pretty much."

If Cameron had been found hanging dead in his garage, would everyone assume that was why? His gaze turned to the house. Paramedics were lifting Cameron onto a stretcher. Rupert hurried down the driveway toward them.

"Good news is that our boy is conscious." He ran one hand over his white beard. And Casey thanked God softly under her breath. "But you were right— he's got some kind of sedative in his system and his windpipe is pretty badly bruised. He tried to talk, but between the windpipe and drugs, he couldn't get much out. We're taking him to the medical center now, but the paramedics are confident he'll bounce back just fine. I'm thankful you guys got here when you did."

"Amen to that," Finnick said.

Rupert leaned in the window toward Casey. "Have you been able to get through to Eileen or David? Because we've tried and haven't gotten any answer."

"They're probably at the ice-skating event," Casey said. "We'll go. I think she should hear this from me."

Rupert nodded. "Tell them to meet us at the medical center."

"Will do."

Casey switched back into the driver's seat for the trip to the skating event. The outdoor rink had been constructed by the volunteer firefighters. Wooden boards squared off a circle of frozen lake just off the shore. Strings of dazzling lights crisscrossed over the skaters as they laughed and swirled, while on the beach, people gathered around the bonfire, sipping hot chocolate. In a dim patch of light, a little ways down from the skating, she could see a handful of people ice fishing. Casey pulled her van to a stop between two vehicles at the edge of the cliff, overlooking the festivities below.

"There's a closer parking lot below," she said. "But it'll be crammed and it's faster to just run. Hang on. I'll be right back."

She got out and slammed the door. Finnick sat in the van and waited as she disappeared down a narrow path. From the back seat, he could hear Nippy grumbling under his breath and sniffing the air as if the dog was bothered by something.

"You okay, buddy?" Finnick asked. "I'll take you for a run when we get back home, okay?"

Home.

He'd been referring to Casey's farmhouse—almost a six-hour drive from where he was going to set up his team—and he'd just called it home.

Within moments, Casey was back with a panicked-looking Eileen and David. He watched as Casey hugged them both in turn. Then her sister and brother-in-law hopped in their car, which was thankfully parked nearby, and disappeared down the road. Casey got back in the van.

"Do you want to go with them?" Finnick asked.

"No," Casey said. "I think they need some time alone with their son. Besides, do you see that little line of lights over there? Those are cars crossing the bridge onto the island." She pointed and he followed her gaze to where a slow trickle of tiny lights were moving west. "The social worker might be at the house soon. I need to get Joey fed and packed before then." She frowned as if an unsettling thought had crossed her mind. "You said the Creepy Shepherd sighting from before turned out to be Tristan. Did you and Patrick talk about what happened to Stella and Tim?" Casey asked.

"Yeah," Finnick said. "His version of the story is that everybody thought it was him because he was declared a person of interest, and he's felt like the cloud of suspicion has stopped him from ever being able to move on with his life."

"I know how he feels." Casey sighed. For a moment, her eyes seemed lost in the darkness. Then she turned to face him. "There's something I need to tell you. My mind hasn't changed on Tim, even with everything your team has found. But—" the word hung on her tongue for a moment, as she pulled in a deep breath and let it out again "—but I'm going to give you whatever you need to petition the court to have his death overturned."

Then, to his surprise, she reached for his hand and grabbed it. He enveloped it in both of his and held it tightly.

"Are you sure?" he asked.

"Yes." She nodded. He could barely see

her features in the darkness, and yet, he knew every line of her face just by memory alone. "Not because I believe he's alive or has done anything wrong," she added. "But because I trust you and your team to find the truth, once and for all, and I'm not going to stand in the way of that."

"I promise you can trust me."

"I know." Casey leaned toward him and her forehead touched his. "I don't feel like I know very much about anything right now. But I know who you are, Ethan Finnick. You are the kindest, strongest, bravest man I've ever met and I trust you with my life."

Something choked in his throat. Her hand slid from his fingers up to his neck. He reached for her and cupped her face in his palms. Slowly and gently, their lips drifted closer.

Nippy barked sharply. They leaped apart.

"What's up?" Finnick turned around and looked at his partner.

Nippy sniffed and shook his head in frustration. His snout snapped the air as if trying to taste it.

"What's going on?" Casey asked.

"He thinks he smells something...but he's not sure."

Casey looked out over the festive scene below.

"What do you mean, he thinks he smells something but isn't sure?" she asked. "You mean there might a body here?"

Finnick was already taking his seat belt off and climbing out of the van.

"Well-trained dogs like Nippy can smell things a mile away and forty feet underground," he said, "from moments after death to up to thirty years later. But sometimes a scent is too faint for them to detect or it gets mixed up with another odor." Nippy leaped out of the van. Finnick ran his hand over the back of the dog's head. "Not to mention, Nippy's getting old and it could just be a dead fish. Not that I've ever known him to get it wrong."

He signaled Nippy to sit and then clipped his leash on.

"Show me," Finnick said. Nippy barked loudly and ran toward the top of the path that led down to the lake, only to stop when he reached the end of his leash. The K-9 barked again. Finnick blew out a long breath. "He definitely thinks he detects something."

"Hang on," Casey said, "I'm coming with you."

Cold wind whipped their faces as they made their way down the path to the ice-skating rink, and she was thankful she'd decided to take the extra moment to zip Joey up in his chest carrier inside her jacket, where he could shelter from the cold.

They moved slowly. Nippy seemed far less confident than he'd been when they'd tracked Ally to the shed. He sniffed both sides of the path, checking out the snow-covered rocks and trees, and often came to a dead stop to snap at the air, as if trying to bite at the scent. As they reached the bottom of the hill, Nippy led them away from the warmth and lights of the skaters, along a darker and narrower path at the base of the cliff. They walked single file. Pools of ice from the lake mingled with the sharp rocks beneath their feet. After a few minutes, lights from the ice fishing huts shone to their left.

"Hey! Stop!" A voice rose from out on the lake. "You can't go that way!"

They looked to see a tall man in a red Canadian-flag ski mask coming over to them. A volunteer firefighter's badge flashed in his hand. He pulled up his mask as he reached them. It was Patrick.

"Hey!" Finnick raised a hand in greeting. "Where's Tristan?"

"Skating with his friends from youth group," Patrick said. "I figured I'd give him an evening off from having to hang with his dad. I'm sorry, but I can't let you walk along the coast. It's not safe."

"The dog thinks he detects something that way," Finnick said, with a shrug. "Do you happen to have any shipwrecks off these cliffs?"

Patrick shook his head. "We don't let boats go that way. It's completely blocked off from the public because the rocks are sharp and the current is nasty. We don't even let people hike in the area above it because there are way too many places to find yourself falling off a cliff and drowning."

Nippy woofed at Finnick impatiently.

Finnick pointed at his partner. "Well, the dog says there's a crime that way."

"Yeah, I heard him." Patrick ran his hand over his face. "Okay, I can load you up on my snowmobile and take you over. I know how to travel it safely and keep you from falling through the ice. But I think we should take Casey and the baby back.

It's really treacherous and the wind's not helping."

Finnick turned to Casey.

"It's okay," she told him quickly, before he'd ever opened his mouth. "I've got to go feed Joey and it is getting colder. Plus, the social worker is coming. You guys stay safe and I'll see you back at the house."

Finnick paused a long moment as if debating what she was saying. But she was right, and he knew it. Still, to Nippy's frustration, Finnick insisted that they all walk her back to the van together. She slid Joey into the car seat and prepared to climb back into the driver's seat.

Then she turned to face Finnick.

"Promise that if you find anything you'll call or text me immediately," Casey said. "Even if it's bad. Even if it's about Tim."

Finnick sighed. "I get what you're saying, but in my experience it's usually easier on people to get bad news in person and when they're not alone."

"Maybe," Casey cut him off. "I don't

know. But right now I can't think of anything worse than worrying and waiting. For over a decade, the emotional pain of not knowing has been the hardest part. And I don't want to feel the pain of not knowing the truth for a single second longer than I have to. Please."

She watched as Finnick swallowed hard. His arms slid open like he was about to hug her. Instead, he crossed them.

"Okay," he said. "I will. I promise."

Then she got in and drove down the narrow, winding highway back toward her home. Indistinct shadows of trees, snowbanks and farmhouses moved past her windows in a blur of grays. Joey began to fuss for a bottle. For a long moment, worries swirled around her mind—from Cameron, to Ally, to Tim and Stella, to whoever's scent Finnick and Nippy were now tracking. But after a few minutes, they all had to take a back seat to a sudden and more pressing problem. Her gas level was dropping quickly. She'd still had over two-thirds of a tank when she left the house that morning, having been sure to fill up just before the snowstorm hit. But now the needle had sunk well into the danger zone, as if her gas tank had sprung a leak and had been draining as she drove. As she started to pray that the van would make it back to town, her vehicle coasted to a stop and died on the side of the road.

Her heart sank. Casey climbed out and scanned the road in each direction. Towering rocks and trees surrounded her on all sides. It was hard to tell exactly where she was in the darkness, but if she had to guess, she was still several miles from town. She pulled out her phone. And couldn't get a signal.

Help me, Lord! Her eyes rose to the dark sky above as worry, frustration and fear all battled for dominion over her heart. *Help me get Joey home!*

Then she saw headlights piercing the darkness. And a green van was pulling up alongside her. Sophie, Lily and Molly, their cheeks still flushed and rosy from ice-skating, waved to her from the back seat.

Jessica stopped the vehicle, then leaned over the empty front seat and pushed the passenger door open.

"You okay?" she asked. "Do you need a ride?"

Casey scanned the four smiling blondes in the van and then felt silly for feeling suspicious.

"Yeah, we ran out of gas," Casey said, leaving out the bit about the fact she might have been sabotaged, "and I've gotta get Joey home for a bottle. Would you mind dropping us off at my house on the way into town?"

Jessica patted the passenger seat. "No problem, I'd be happy to."

They buckled Joey's car seat into the middle seat behind Jessica, and the three girls gathered around him, jiggling his toys and cooing as they drove down the narrow highway back to town.

As they reached Juniper Cove's first stop sign, Jessica angled the rearview mirror to glance at them before she started driving again.

"I'm actually really glad I ran into you," Jessica said. She swiped one hand up and down her arm self-consciously, and then snapped it back to the wheel. "I just really wanted to apologize to you for that whole mix-up back at the pageant earlier. I don't know how I got it in my head that you'd said it was okay for Sophie to hold Joey for a few pictures, but I didn't mean to put anybody on the spot."

"It's no problem," Casey said. "I'm sure next year everyone will have a completely new Christmas pageant–related catastrophe to gossip about."

Jessica laughed subconsciously and adjusted her sleeves.

"Well, I'm really glad that everything is okay between us." She pulled the van to a stop. "I'd hate if there were any bad feelings between us."

"Don't worry. It's all good," Casey said.

She looked up and realized that Jessica had stopped in front of her own house first, instead of taking Casey and Joey home. The lights were on and Drew's van was in the driveway. At least Casey now had a phone signal. She sent Finnick a quick text, telling him where she was.

Jessica leaned over and slid open the back door. "Come on, girls! Daddy is waiting for you and has got the living room all set up!"

The girls gave Joey sweet hugs and kisses goodbye, then they ran off squealing into the house. Jessica closed the back door again.

"Drew is doing a special movie night for the girls tonight," Jessica said, and again that self-conscious twinge was back in her voice. "He's got a sheet set up for a screen, and he's going to play a movie off his laptop onto the digital projector. He created a whole fort of blankets and pillows on the floor so they can curl up and sleep there tonight. And he's made them hot chocolate and popcorn and everything."

Casey nodded, not quite sure why the other woman was telling her all this. It sounded like she was trying very hard to convince Casey that Drew was a good father. And the longer she talked, the more she fidgeted with her clothes.

"It sounds lovely," Casey said.

"Do you want to come in for a tea or something before you go?" Jessica asked.

"No, I'm sorry," Casey said. "Another time, please. I have to take Joey home and feed him his bottle."

"Oh, we have bottles for him," Jessica said, quickly, "clothes, formula and everything. Even a brand new crib."

Casey blinked. "I didn't know you guys were expecting a baby."

She smiled at the younger woman. But Jessica didn't smile back. Instead, worry filled her eyes.

"Look, I'm not supposed to tell anybody about this yet..." Jessica said. "But Drew has almost sorted everything out with social services, and you know what gossip is like on this island. So I wanted to make sure that you heard it from me first."

"Heard what?"

"We're adopting Joey," Jessica said. "Drew's talked to social services and it's all taken care of. We're going to be Joey's new family."

TEN

Finnick's phone pinged in his pocket.

He was sitting on the back seat of Patrick's snowmobile, with a large pile of ice-fishing equipment on the rack behind him, and Nippy trotting alongside, still on his leash, as the snowmobile matched the dog's slow pace.

Finnick braced against the wind, pulled his cell out and glanced at the screen. It was Casey. Telling him she'd run out of gas at the side of the road and was now at Drew and Jessica's house. He texted her back to keep him posted.

"Hang on!" Patrick called. "There's a very sharp turn up ahead. I can't remember the official name for it, but there's a channel between two cliffs. The local kids used to call it Daredevil Point and we'd egg each other on to jump off it into the lake."

"How many times did you do it?" Finnick called back.

Patrick laughed.

"Only once," he returned. "When I was twelve. One of the friends that Drew and I were with landed badly and broke his leg in three places. After that, there was still a lot of talk but kids moved their stupid stunts to a slightly safer place." They rounded the corner. The channel was about the width of an ice hockey rink. Sheer rock faces towered high on every side. Patrick shook his head. "Can I tell you a secret? Drew never jumped off the cliff that day but still ran around telling everyone he did."

Nippy barked sharply and tugged on the leash.

"I think we're there," Finnick called.

Patrick pulled the snowmobile to a stop

near the cliff. Finnick hopped off and ran his hand over Nippy's head.

"Good job," he said. "Show me what you've found."

Nippy barked, ran over to a patch of the ice in the center of the channel and started to dig. His paws slipped uselessly on the ice.

"I've got something that can cut through that if you want," Patrick called.

"Sure, thanks."

Finnick called Nippy to heel and ran another grateful hand over the dog's head. "Whatever was buried out here under the ice," he told Nippy, "I think you're the only one who could've found it."

Patrick pulled an auger from his gear on the back of the snowmobile and jammed it into the ice where Nippy had been scratching. The drill was long, thin and the size of a pogo stick. The screeching sound of ice-cutting filled the air as Patrick drilled down into the frozen surface a couple of feet until he reached water and then he stepped back. Finnick grabbed a giant flashlight off the snowmobile and shone it down into the water below. The light hit on something red and metallic under the water. The ice was even thicker here than where Patrick had been icefishing.

"What is that?" Patrick asked.

"I'm not sure yet," Finnick said. But an unsettling picture was beginning to form in his mind as to what the red object could be. And judging by the worry lines that creased Patrick's forehead, he suspected the same thought had crossed the other man's mind too.

An odd and heavy silence began to fall between them as Patrick continued to dig, punching a hole after hole in the ice, breaking it up into giant blocks that Finnick could then, with the help of ice hooks, wrench out.

Now it was crystal clear what Nippy had found buried under the ice, and neither man needed the other one to say it.

It was Tim's car, slipped on its side and

submerged under water, with the remains of two people in the front seat, still buckled in their seat belts.

Finnick stepped back from the wreck, pulled out his phone and checked the screen. Casey still hadn't texted. Nippy leaned against his leg. Finnick reached down his free hand and ran his fingers through the comforting fur of the amazing partner who'd been by his side for the past twelve years. "I hope you know how incredibly proud of you I am," he said softly.

Then he pulled his phone from his pocket and placed a call to the Ontario police commissioner Isaac Cannon. Despite the fact it was after work hours on Christmas Eve, Commissioner Cannon answered on the first ring.

"Sir, we've located Tim Thompson's car with two bodies inside," Finnick said. "I think we finally discovered them."

His work here was done, Finnick thought, when he'd finished relaying the pertinent details to the commissioner and ended the call. It was all in the hands of the RCMP now. They'd coordinate with island police, send an expert team to cordon off the area, extract the car, retrieve the bodies inside and officially confirm what a still, small voice inside Finnick's heart already knew—Tim and Stella had finally been found.

He tried to call Casey and when he couldn't get through, he texted her, knowing that she would want to know as soon as possible to put her mind at rest immediately.

I think Nippy found them.

He heard the sound of Patrick's auger drill clattering against the ice and turned back. The man's hands had clenched into fists and he looked angry enough to punch a hole straight through the cliff's side. Patrick turned to the sky and a roar of anger and pain ripped through his lips. Then his shoulders slumped like a man defeated and he faced Finnick.

"This is all my fault," Patrick said.

"I'm sure it isn't," Finnick said. "After all, you brought me here."

"But I should've known." Patrick ran both hands over his head. "The day before Stella vanished she came into work and asked me for help. She showed me these bruises on her arms, the size of fingerprints, and told me that Drew was hurting her. She asked me to take her to the mainland so she could go to a police station that wasn't on the island and get help. And so help me, I didn't believe her." He groaned. "Drew told me that she was lying," Patrick said, "and I believed him. He was my best friend and he'd convinced me that Stella had a habit of exaggerating and making things up. I also believed him when he told me he'd heard somebody say Stella and Tim had been spotted in Tim's car in Sudbury."

"So, Drew was the one who started that rumor?" Finnick asked.

"I think so," Patrick said. "Maybe. When

he married Jessica, she seemed so happy. I couldn't believe he'd ever hurt her. But what Stella had said never totally left me. I stayed close to the family and kept an eye on them all these years. Just for any signs of trouble. But the little girls seemed so happy and I just couldn't imagine he'd hurt anyone. But what if Drew killed Tim and Stela, and then hurt Jessica, and it's my fault he never got caught?"

Fear washed over Finnick like a wave. "Casey and Joey are at Drew and Jessica's house now."

Patrick turned and ran back toward the snowmobile, with Finnick and Nippy just one step behind.

"And it's not your fault," Finnick added. "Predators are really good at hiding who they are. If Drew did hide a nasty side of himself from you, it's probably because he knew that you'd try to stop him."

He just prayed it wasn't too late to stop him now.

* * *

Three mini marshmallows danced in the mug of hot chocolate sitting in front of Casey on the Thatcher family's kitchen table. Joey sat in a soft baby-lounger chair on the floor, stubbornly refusing his bottle. Finnick's last text burned like a fire in Casey's mind.

Lord, have they really found Tim's and Stella's bodies? Is this nightmare finally over?

Joy and hope filled her heart and she thanked God for Finnick's text. Everything inside her wanted to text him back. No, wanted to run out the door, all the way to where Finnick was, throw her arms around him in joy and relief. Instead, here she was stuck at the Thatcher's kitchen table waiting for Jessica to give her and Joey a ride back to her farmhouse. Casey's vehicle was still stranded without gas at the side of the road. The island didn't have a taxi service and it would be a long walk home in the cold with the baby. She still hadn't seen Drew—or the kids again—since they'd come home. But Jessica had told her that he had made both the hot chocolate and Joey's bottle especially for them.

More importantly, she still didn't know why Jessica and Drew thought they were going to adopt Joey. An eerie feeling began to climb up her spine. *The social worker had told her that Joey was going to be with his father...*

Jessica walked in, sat and downed her drink.

"Is everything okay with your hot chocolate?" Jessica asked, anxiously.

"Yeah." Casey took a sip. "It's wonderful. I'm just not really into sweet things, due to all the sweet-smelling stuff I'm surrounded by in my workshop every day. Chocolate peppermint was my bestselling soap this year. And for Easter, I'm going to make soaps that look like marshmallow bunnies."

She gave up trying to offer the bottle

to Joey and shook it. There was sediment in the bottom, like it hadn't been mixed very well. She dropped it into Joey's diaper bag.

Jessica ran her hands over her eyes and yawned. She looked ready to pass out at the table and Casey wondered how many sleepless nights she'd had. She couldn't imagine what Jessica was going through and compassion flooded her heart.

"Hey, it's okay." Casey reached across the table and took her hands. "I'm sure this whole situation with Joey must be really overwhelming. But when the social worker told me that Joey's father had come forward and that his family was going to raise him—"

"Drew's not Joey's father," Jessica said sharply. She pulled her hands away. "He just told CPS that he was. But only because he had to. But…but they know he's lying, because he'd never do anything like that."

"What?" Casey shook her head like there was water in her ears.

"See, the real father is a young man who Drew was, um…mentoring on his business trips." Jessica sounded like she was dutifully repeating a script that she didn't believe a word of. "And…and the guy can't raise a baby. So Drew agreed to pretend to be Joey's dad."

"The adoption system doesn't work that way," Casey said, softly. "He has to go through a whole bunch of steps to prove that—"

"Well, it *has* to work that way," Jessica cut her off. "Because Drew always says he has the perfect family and he would never do anything to jeopardize that."

Before Casey could say another word, Jessica dropped her head onto her arms and began to cry.

Lord, please comfort her and be her rescue.

Casey leaped from her seat, ran around the table and laid a comforting hand on

Jessica's back. "Hey, it's going to be okay. You're really strong, this community loves you and God can do incredible things. But right now, I've got to get back home."

And talk to Finnick about all of this.

Fear crawled up her spine. She didn't know why Drew was lying, she just knew she had to get herself and Joey out of this house.

Jessica's tears turned to soft whimpers and then stopped. But her head didn't rise. Casey stepped back. Jessica's eyes had closed. Casey reached for her shoulder and Jessica's head lolled over to the side. She'd passed out at the table. A warning bell sounded in Casey's head.

"Hey...you okay?" she asked, giving the woman a gentle shake. "You've fallen asleep at the table."

No answer. She reached for the woman's wrist and it flopped limply in her hand.

Now the warning in her head had gone to a full-fledged siren, clanging along with her pounding heart. She threw the diaper bag over her shoulder, scooped Joey up into her arms and ran through the room and into the hall. The movie still danced on a sheet in the living room. But all three girls had fallen asleep, curled up on the blankets and pillows Drew had laid out for them. Casey picked up a fallen mug from the floor. There was some kind of powdered sediment in the bottom.

Was it spiked with something? Thankfully Casey had only had one sip of her drink and Joey had refused to touch his.

"Come on, Joey." She ran for the door. "We're going to get out of here and go get help."

She opened the door and felt the cold wind hit her face. Darkness and snow filled her eyes. She fumbled for her phone and texted Finnick, praying that he'd receive her messages and would send help.

The floorboards creaked behind her. Something sharp pressed deep into the small of her back.

"Going somewhere, sweet pea?" A dark

and gritty voice that she'd remember from her nightmares filled her ear. He snatched the phone from her hand and threw it to the floor. Joey cried softly and Casey hugged him closer to her.

Drew spun her around and she stared into a smile as wide and lifeless as the mask he'd worn over the past few days.

"So, you're the one who's been dressing up as the Creepy Shepherd all this time?" Casey asked. Drew smirked and nodded. "Why would you do that?"

"Thought it was funny," Drew said with a self-satisfied shrug. "I couldn't find Ally and the baby. I needed to see if they were with you. I needed a disguise and there it was."

"So, you killed Ally?" she pressed. "Why?"

She was stalling him now, trying to buy time for Finnick to reach her and hoping that a man who was grandiose enough to try to take people's lives while dressed as a shepherd, could be lured into bragging about his crimes. Her phone began to ring. Drew stomped on it hard and it fell silent. That's when it hit her—he was dressed to go outside.

"Ally was a nobody and a nothing," Drew snarled. "She never even knew my real name."

"Because you told her that you were my long-lost Tim," Casey said, "and she believed you."

He chuckled. "That was clever, wasn't it? Making fake IDs in Tim's name, letting people think he was out in the world getting into trouble."

"No, that was just gross." Casey cradled Joey closer, as for a moment, disgust at his crimes overcame her fear. "So you killed Ally because you didn't want anyone to find out about the sick little game you were playing those two weekends a month you went away 'on business.'"

Drew scowled. "She tried to blackmail me for money, and said if I didn't give it to her she'd tell everyone that Tim Thompson was Joey's father."

"Which meant people might find out it was really you," Casey said. "She threatened me too, but I didn't kill her."

"Instead you took my baby!" Drew's voice rose.

"I protected him!" Casey's voice rose too. "From you! A man who wanted to kill him! And then, what? You set out to kill me and Finnick for protecting him? And my nephew, why?"

"She sent an email to Cameron the night she died and then deleted it from her phone."

Ally...

Cameron's last word to her before Drew had attacked him filled her mind. What had Cameron been trying to tell her?

"Why?"

"I don't know!" Drew shook his head as if he was angry that she didn't understand and appreciate how clever he was and the corner he'd felt backed into. But it wasn't that she didn't understand. It's that she didn't care. "As I told your friend, I'm not about to let anyone mess with my perfect family."

"You drugged your family!"

"And they fell asleep, peacefully and happily!" Drew shouted. "And now they're never going to wake up and know that Ally was trying to blackmail me for money for the kid. Or that if anyone ever did a DNA test on Joey they'd find out he was mine. I tried to get my hands on Joey and kill him along with his mother. But now, you've left me with no choice but to wipe the slate clean and start a new life on this island. But I'll be fine. I got so much love and sympathy from people on this island when they thought Stella left me. I know I'll be okay. Which is more than I can say for you. You're going to wish you drank that hot chocolate because you're going to wish you were sleeping through what happens next."

Before she could even think about how

to fight him off, he grabbed her by the neck, shoved her hard across the floor and threw her into the closet. She tumbled inside, sheltering Joey in her arms.

The door slammed and a lock clicked shut. Minutes ticked past and for a long time Casey couldn't hear anything but the sound of her own fist banging on the wood and her own voice calling for help.

Then she smelled smoke.

ELEVEN

"Friends of yours?" Patrick asked. His hands tightened on the steering wheel of his van as his eyes darted up to the rearview mirror. "Don't look now, but I think we're being followed. We picked them up after we passed the turn off to Casey's farmhouse."

Finnick glanced over his shoulder, past where Nippy now sat at attention on the back seat of Patrick's van. Sure enough, not one but two sets of headlights seemed to be following them at every turn.

Either that or they were in a big hurry to get to Drew and Jessica's too.

"I don't know," Finnick said, "but there are two of them."

He, Nippy and Patrick had raced back

to Patrick's van on the snowmobile, this time with Nippy cradled awkwardly on Finnick's lap. They'd peeled off in Patrick's van soon after, as the younger man pressed his vehicle through faster speeds and sharper turns than Finnick would have dared. And now the two mystery vehicles on their tail were matching their every move.

Finnick tried Casey's number over and over again, fear rising higher in his throat each time it went through to voicemail. His logical brain tried to tell him that the thirtieth call would be no different from the twenty-ninth, and that she'd pick up if she could. But something inside his heart wouldn't let him stop.

Lord, I need Casey to be alive. I don't want to envision a life without her.

Patrick had rolled his window down a crack, sending a stream of wintery air whipping through the cab, producing a similar effect to a cold slap in the face. But as they neared Drew and Jessica's house, something even more troubling slipped in through the gap—the smell of something burning.

Finnick watched as Patrick's face went white and somehow the volunteer fire chief managed to push the van even faster.

Small pellets of ice and rocks kicked up under his tires as Patrick swerved into the driveway. Smoke billowed out from under the attached garage door. Bright orange flames shot out of the home's windows.

"I installed their smoke-detector system myself!" Patrick yelled, as he slammed on the brakes and jumped out. "Where is everybody—firefighters from across the island should be converging here now!"

He snapped his phone to his ear and began shouting to someone from Dispatch. Finnick leaped out the passenger door. Nippy bounded over the middle console and followed him into the snow.

He steeled a breath and stared up at the house.

Where do I start? Where do I run? What do I do?

Lord, I can't do this alone.

The van and car that had been tailing them pulled into the driveway on either side.

"Hey, boss!" Jackson leaped out of the van, followed by his K-9 German shepherd, Hudson. Gemma got out of the passenger seat. Caleb, Lucas and Lucas's yellow Lab, Michigan, jumped out of the car as well. "How can we help?"

Finnick pulled in a deep breath as a prayer of thanksgiving filled his lungs. "How did you find me?"

"That's all Michigan," Lucas ran one hand down his arson-detecting K-9's side. "We'd just arrived at Casey's house and she started barking up a storm. So, we left Amy and Skye there, and went to see what he was making such a fuss about."

Patrick was still on the phone with Dispatch to get every able-bodied person on the island to the Thatcher house.

"Jackson, I need you and Hudson to track the criminal who I think set this fire," Finnick ordered. "Something tells me we won't find him here. You should be able to get a scent from something in that van. Gemma, stay out here and co-ordinate with civilians as they arrive. We might need some really good crowd control. Caleb, Lucas and Michigan, you're with me."

Together the three men and the arson K-9 ran for the front door. The fire seemed to have been started in the garage and was moving to the main part of the house. The front door was locked, but even as Caleb was preparing to throw his shoulder into it, Patrick rushed up, wielding a fire axe.

They smashed the door open. Thick, acrid smoke filled Finnick's lungs and stung his eyes.

"We've got three children on the floor!" Lucas shouted, making a beeline for the girls. "They're breathing but unconscious. Help me get them all outside."

Lucas, Caleb and Patrick scooped the three girls up into their arms and carried them out of the building into the snow, where Gemma was waiting.

"Casey!" Finnick shouted. "Casey, where are you?"

For a moment, all he heard was the sizzle, cracking and popping sound of the fire moving closer and closer across the house toward him.

Then he heard a faint voice calling his name.

"Finnick! Joey and I are in here!"

"I'm coming!" He ran for the closet nearby. The door seemed to be locked, but when he leveled a good hard kick at the frame, it cracked and came free. He yanked the door open.

There was Casey, down on the ground, sheltering Joey in her arms. He knelt beside her.

"Finnick?" Her voice was weak. She coughed. "Is it really you?"

"Yeah, it's me." His voice grew husky

in his throat. "Come on, let's get you out of here."

Suddenly he felt Patrick by his side, gently scooping Joey up out of Casey's arms and carrying the precious cargo outdoors at a run. Finnick slid his arms under Casey's back and legs. She wrapped her arms around him and cradled herself to his chest, and he hustled her out of the fire and into the snow, just in time to see Lucas carrying Jessica out and over to her girls.

"Tell the paramedics that the children and Jessica were drugged," Casey called faintly to Patrick.

"Got it!" Patrick shouted.

He disappeared into the crowd with Joey. Suddenly it was like the entire town of Juniper Cove and a quarter of the rest of the island descended on the house at once, setting up bucket chains and hoses pouring bucket after bucket of water on the burning house, as they worked together to save it. Paramedics and friends gathered around Jessica and the three girls, keeping them warm and safe as they slowly regained consciousness and woke up, no doubt overwhelmed by the chaos around them.

And Finnick walked through it all with Casey tucked safely in his arms.

"Did you really find Tim and Stella?" she asked.

"Yeah," he said. "Their remains still need to be officially identified, but my heart tells me it's them."

"Where were they?"

"Under the water at Daredevil Point."

She sighed and nestled deeper into his neck. He carried her over to where an empty bench lay, at the edge of the action.

"Drew was the Creepy Shepherd," she said. "He drugged his family and there should be evidence of what he used in Joey's baby bottle in my diaper bag. He's been using Tim's identity to cheat on his wife, and was willing to kill Ally, Joey, you, me and his entire family to maintain that perfect image."

She shuddered.

"He won't get away with it, I promise," Finnick said.

He sat down on the bench, expecting her to slide off onto the seat beside him. Instead, she stayed curled up against him, with her arms gently around his shoulders and his around her body. Nippy galloped over to them and sat by their feet.

"Thank you for finding me, Finnick," Casey whispered.

"I had a lot of help," he said. "From Patrick and my team. The woman with short dark hair currently hugging Jessica is my civilian coordinator and private detective, Gemma Locke. The man with dark hair at the front of the bucket brigade is Lucas. His golden Lab, Michigan, is the one who alerted them to the fire. And the blond, unhandsome man talking to Rupert is Caleb."

She laughed.

"I recognize them from the video call," Casey said. "What are they doing here?"

"I think they're here to surprise me for Christmas," Finnick said. "I promised them I'd have dinner with them tonight. I guess they decided to bring dinner to me."

"Hey, boss!" Jackson's voice called from behind them. "Is this the guy you are looking for?"

Casey slid off Finnick's lap, and they both stood to see Jackson and Hudson emerge from the trees with a very angry and muddy-looking Drew handcuffed between them.

"Yup, that's him," Finnick said.

Hudson woofed triumphantly.

"We found him wandering down the road with the most fantastical story to tell," Jackson said, with a laugh. "Apparently, his house caught fire, and although he valiantly tried to save his beloved wife and daughters, the fire was just too strong and he had no choice but to flee and try to find help!"

Finnick snorted. "Take him over to the man with the big white beard talking to Caleb and tell him Christmas has come early."

"Right on!" Jackson escorted his prisoner over to Rupert.

Finnick turned to Casey.

"Can you hang tight here for a moment?" he asked. "I need to go coordinate things with my team. Knowing Gemma, I suspect she's already gotten Jessica to agree to cooperate. But even if not, we should have enough to go on to get Drew Thatcher put away for the rest of his life. And that's even before we're able to talk to Cameron and find out what he'd wanted to tell you about Ally before he was attacked."

As he said the words, he saw two women in jeans, jackets and large laminated badges on lanyards coming toward them.

"That's my social worker and I'm guessing Joey's caseworker," she said. "I need to go talk to them and say goodbye to Joey."

Finnick felt his eyes widen. "Why would you have to say goodbye to Joey?" Everything inside him balked at the thought. "There's no way they're going to let Drew take custody of him after what he tried to do..."

"I know," Casey said. "But it may be months, or even years, before the court manages to revoke his parental rights. Until then, he'll probably be placed with a relative of Drew's or Ally's, if they can find one to take him. There's a big, long process here, and the fact he was placed in my manger doesn't mean I get to keep him."

Finnick scanned the crowd for Joey but couldn't manage to find the little boy.

"Hey, it's okay." Casey slid her hand to Finnick's face and turned him toward her. He saw the sadness in his own heart echoed in her eyes. "I always knew I was only a temporary, emergency caregiver.

There are thousands of families wanting to adopt and only a few hundred infants ever come up for adoption a year. But have faith that God will guide Joey's life from here and place him into the arms of the right family who will love him forever. Meanwhile, I'll try to open my heart to whatever adventure and child God brings me next."

But, you and Joey belong together! The words burst through his heart, but he didn't let them pass his lips.

"Hey, not all happy endings are instant," Casey said, apparently reading the hesitation on his face. "Some of them take a really, really, *really* long time, especially with adoption and fostering. I promise, it's going to be okay, in God's time."

Before he could even try to find words to say, she reached up and kissed him on the temple, then turned away. She made her way through the crowd, leaving him standing there watching her go.

Lord, all this time I thought I was rescu-

ing Casey. But now I see that in some ways she's stronger than I feel like I could be.

"You okay, boss?" Gemma walked toward him. There was a curious look on the private eye's face, as if she was seeing more than he was intending to show.

"We've solved the crime and caught the criminal," Finnick said, "and I can't believe you're all here to be a part of it."

"To be fair, our plan was just to surprise you for Christmas Eve dinner while Lucas repaired your windshield," she said.

"Well, sometimes everything just comes together perfectly," Finnick said.

And sometimes exactly the opposite was true.

Gemma stood beside him and watched as Casey disappeared into the crowd.

"I wish I could say that we'll all be fine without you," Gemma said, as if she'd read something deeper in his eyes than he'd even figured out yet how to put into words. "But that wouldn't be true. Our task force only exists because of all your hard work to make it happen, and if you walk away from it now, I don't know how long it will take for someone or something else to step up and take its place. If anything or anyone ever does."

The private detective had always been so incredibly perceptive.

Finnick turned to face her. "Why are you telling me all this?"

"Because I want you to know that I mean it when I say that as much as every single one of us loves this work and can't wait to get started," Gemma said, "we'll understand if you decide to let the task force go."

Bright Christmas morning sunshine beamed upon Casey's face and dazzled the snow around her as she walked down the narrow path that Finnick had dug between her house and the road. Behind her, the farmhouse was full of more people, joy and activity than she'd ever seen before. Caleb, Lucas and Jackson—along with Hudson and Michigan—had bunked out in the garage with Finnick and Nippy overnight, while Gemma, Amy and her baby, Skye, had stayed with Casey in the house.

Now they were all crowded in her living room and kitchen, coordinating a breakfast out of the remains of what she'd bought at the market and the bags full of groceries the team had had the foresight to bring. And she'd stepped outside to pray.

She took a deep breath and felt the winter air fill her lungs.

How many times have I prayed that You fill this house with people, laughter and joy? And today You have answered my prayers in ways that I never imagined.

A door creaked open and then shut behind her. Footsteps crunched on the snow.

"May I join you?" Finnick asked.

She reached out her hand for him without turning back. He took it. And together they looked out at the morning sky.

"I heard Cameron has already been released from the hospital and will make a full recovery," Finnick said.

"He has," Casey said. "Eileen called me late last night and said they'd see me today."

"Gemma has already managed to get Drew's picture in front of multiple people who are willing to testify that he was the 'Tim' who was dating Ally," Finnick said. "They got the car out of the water last night and fast-tracked the dental record identification overnight. Now, the bodies in the water have been positively iden-tified as Tim and Stella, thanks to their dental records. Patrick has already given a full statement to police."

"Your team is absolutely incredible," she said.

"I know," Finnick said, "which is why I can't leave them. No matter how much something in my heart desperately wishes I could stay here with you—"

"Finnick." She turned toward him. "*I'm* not staying here. I don't know where I'm going to move to, but it's time for me to sell this place and move off the island. All this time, I've been holding on to Tim's dream of raising a family here and trying to make it a reality. But it's time for me to go and find my own dream." Slowly, she pulled her hand from his and wrapped her arm around his waist. "I'm not going to be Casey Thompson anymore."

His hands slid along the small of her back and pulled her closer.

"Do you think, one day, you'd be willing to become Casey Finnick?" he asked, softly.

She nodded, feeling happy tears rush to the corners of her eyes. "Yes, I think I'd like that very much."

A long and happy sigh slid from Finnick's lungs. He leaned toward her and his forehead rested against hers. "You are the only home I ever want," he said. "I love you, Casey."

"I love you too."

Slowly, their lips met in a gentle kiss

that grew stronger with every passing heartbeat as he pulled her closer to him and lifted her off her feet.

Then she heard the sound of a car pulling up in front of her house, and her sister, Eileen, called her name. Casey slid slowly out of Finnick's arms and turned around.

Eileen was practically running down the path toward her, tears streaming from her sister's eyes. Casey ran for her and caught her in a hug.

"Eileen?" Casey said. "Are you okay? How's Cameron?"

"He's here," Eileen said. Casey looked over her shoulder. Cameron had stepped out of the car and seemed to be getting something bulky from the back seat. "I'm sorry. It's my fault you never got a foster child."

Casey stepped back as if someone had slapped her. "What? It was your fault?"

"Forgive me, please," Eileen said. "Whenever I got called for a reference, I said I didn't think you were ready. But I was wrong. And either way, it wasn't my place to try to interfere like that."

Then, suddenly, a happy baby's squeal filled the air.

"Joey?"

To Casey's amazement, she turned to see Cameron carefully carrying Joey across the snow toward them. She ran for him, but Finnick reached him first. Cameron slid the little boy into Finnick's strong arms and Casey threw her arms around Finnick and Joey all at once. She brushed a kiss over Joey's face. The baby laughed and pinched her cheek.

She turned to Cameron and Eileen. "I don't understand."

"Joey is my son," Cameron said, his words halting and nervous but shining with truth. "I had a relationship with Ally. But we cut it off when she got pregnant because I was a coward... I was afraid my parents would cut me off and disown me." Eileen sniffed loudly and reached out to grab her son's shoulder. Cameron continued, "So, she lied and told Drew that he was the father, thinking he'd support her financially. That's why I was here outside your house the night you found Joey and ran when you saw me. I knew she was coming here and I wanted to stop her. That's what I was trying to tell you about Ally when Drew attacked me. He suspected that Ally had told me about their relationship."

"Looked like he was trying to tie up all the loose ends," Finnick said.

"That you're Joey's father?" Casey asked, softly.

"Yes, and I have the DNA test to prove it," Cameron said.

She looked to the tiny child in Finnick's arms. "So I'm his great aunt."

"Yes." Cameron stepped away from his mother and grabbed her hand. "But I want him to live here with you. I want you to adopt him and be his mother. And if you want to leave here and go be with Ethan in

Toronto, that's good by me too. It's close to my college and I can visit him all the time." For the first time in a long time, she saw a huge and genuine smile cross Cameron's face. "I love you, Aunt Casey, and you're the best possible mother for Joey. I've talked to my parents, and I know they feel that way too."

Casey glanced to her big sister. Happy tears filled Eileen's eyes. Then Casey threw her arms around her nephew and pulled Eileen and Finnick into the hug, and for a long moment, they held each other in the snow. When they finally pulled apart, Eileen said that she and Cameron had to go get ready for the Christmas service. But they would be back later with David and a mountain of food to join in Christmas dinner with Finnick's team.

Then Finnick, Casey and Joey stood together in the snow and watched as they drove away.

She turned to look at Finnick. A tear

glistened in the corner of his eye, as he cradled Joey to him.

"Are you all right, Finnick?" she asked.

"Better than I've ever been." He turned to face her and love filled his gaze. "Please promise me that you'll marry me, and I'll never have to go a single day—Christmas or otherwise—without you and Joey in my life."

"I promise. I love you, Finnick."

She stood on her tiptoes and kissed him. He kissed her back.

Then they turned toward the farmhouse.

"Don't pretend you're all not watching!" he yelled. "Let Nippy out and come join us!"

Casey laughed, as her farmhouse door opened and Nippy raced out across the snow toward them, followed by the grinning and clapping members of the Cold Case Task Force.

She felt Finnick's hand take hers and hold it tightly. And she knew with complete certainty in her heart that she'd found a life and a love that was deeper, stronger and more glorious than she'd ever imagined.

* * * * *

Dear Reader,

It's been ten years since I wrote my first Love Inspired Suspense. Back then, I had two young children and my Christmas was filled with plays, pageants, brightly wrapped toys and peals of laughter. This year, my kids are grown and will be spending Christmas Day elsewhere with their wonderful cousins. It'll be a quiet Christmas for me this year, but a very good one too.

I've had a lot of different Christmases in my life. I've cut down a real tree, had artificial trees of various sizes and, on more than one year, I decorated a houseplant up with Christmas decorations. I've celebrated Christmas in piles of heavy snow and in sun-drenched South America. One year, when I was away from home in England, I went to a Christmas party that a local church was holding for people who didn't have family. It was really wonderful. And there were some years I celebrated family Christmas on days other than December 25.

This season, I ended up alone when the loved ones I was planning on seeing got sick.

While I was creating Finnick, I had a lot of joy thinking about the kind of man who volunteers to work Christmas Day so that others can be with their families.

It's my hope for you that wherever you are, and whoever you celebrate with, that you'll be surrounded by the knowledge that your life has value and you are endlessly loved by the God who created you.

Merry Christmas and thank you for sharing this journey with me,

Maggie